TIME BOUND

ATHINA FERNWOOD

For all the dreamers and adventurers,
who dare to believe in the impossible.
And for those who remind us that love and destiny know no bounds.
This journey is for you.
Feel free to personalize it further if you have specific people in mind
you'd like to dedicate it to.

Athina Fernwood

PROLOGUE

I t's the year 2025, and everyone knows the world will never be the same.

It has officially been one year since the decline in the birthrate of female children was confirmed across the world.

So much so that many are frantically speculating on the outcomes.

Of course, when scientists first began to realize what was happening, no one was listening.

The news channels were all about political debates, celebrity stories, and weather issues. Though, maybe the environmental changes could have had something to do with what happened.

No one really knows what brought about the pandemic which would change the world.

When awareness finally began to spread, it spread like wildfire. Of course, even then many people did not understand the gravity of the situation or just how quickly it was all happening.

There wasn't much time after that.

Scientists, biologists, and many of the world's smartest minds came together in a panic. They were trying to figure out why, how to stop it, or even what was happening. They should have just been figuring out what was going to happen once they failed at those things.

But they didn't.

Unbeknownst to the world, there were even more changes taking place. Well, at least, as far as they could tell. These other beings may have always been around, hidden from view.

Once the world began to fall apart, though, they became known. Shifters. Beings that could shift from man to creature, and back. Mainly wolves were known; at least in the United States.

Maybe this happened because they were being affected by the strange epidemic of females becoming few and far between. Maybe whatever unknown change in the world that created the epidemic also created them.

This is yet another thing most of the world never got an answer to.

What many did find out, way too quickly, was that the world fell apart fast. Faster than any of them prepared for.

Between widespread panic, the natural death rate, and how long it took people to either become aware or care- certain towns and cities began to crumble.

The first-world countries seemed to be hit first. Maybe it just seemed that way because they were the main places with media coverage.

Everyone took it a different way. Some people moved further away from society while many others moved together, congregating in cities. At least at first.

Then, the shifters were discovered.

Media outlets were constantly focusing on shifters. Some people blamed them, some people said they were a threat because they could take females from them. So, most shifters around the world left any semblance of civilization and chose to live in areas that they would claim as their territory.

It seemed as if humans chose to focus on the different circumstances they could see and forget about the one they could not.

Around the year 2044, the majority of the smaller cities were being abandoned.

Many people still seemed to live in the larger, more well-known cities; perhaps hoping that being around as many people as possible could help them increase their chances of finding a wife. Maybe they just wanted any semblance of normalcy they could still find.

There were still outposts in certain places around the world, like the CDC in the States, where people held out hope for finding anything to make this better.

But more and more people were realizing that their world would never be the same and was choosing to begin their new lives as best they could.

It still somewhat resembled a world many were used to. By then, though, the number of females being born had decreased by a quarter of the amount worldwide.

It became significantly worse once it got to the year 2095. The decrease in women had caused many bloodlines to die off. Civilization began to disappear in certain areas of the world while different ways of life became the new normal.

Modern things that had once been taken for granted were quickly being discarded. Resources were becoming limited, along with manpower. So, many people were being trained and given jobs for things deemed necessary to this new way of life.

Many men became farmers, some took to doing things that would give society gas and oil. Some trained as medics and even teachers, hoping to still provide some civilized future to the newer generations. Many just took care of themselves.

There was still a military- significantly smaller obviously. Its main objectives were communication with other countries, piloting the few planes left when the need was highly necessary, and providing help or safety when the need arose. The latter was important when law and order got extremely out of control. They were run by the little government left and seemed to become more and more used only in bigger populated areas.

Smaller, more rural areas seemed to have their own forms of law. Many men would, for the most part, follow the laws like before. But, like any law, it only worked when the people followed it. As things got progressively worse, it seemed things became more where laws were lines that were there. If someone crossed it, they either got away with it or an individual would have to dole out their own justice.

Something else happened this year that no one had an explanation for. There was a plane crash outside of Chicago. Planes were never really used anymore, unless absolutely necessary, because of how much fuel they use.

But what was even stranger, was the fact that everyone that survived the crash said the year was 2012. Inexplicably, the plane came from the past and carried a total of 53 survivors. 30 of those were women.

It seemed to provide such a significant relief to the struggling population rate, that many societal issues around the country were at a temporary lull as many men were given a new sense of hope.

Shifters, having been living in packs with their internal sense of hierarchy, seemed to become more civilized as humans became less as the years passed.

Each pack was led by an Alpha, Beta, and Delta. There were, of course, different positions in each pack. They would protect each other and their territory; many even forming shaky alliances with humans around them.

Essentially, they would follow society's rules when out of

their territory unless they were threatened. No one would harm their territory or them without repercussions. It worked, for the most part, because everyone knew they were no match for the shifters.

Some packs even had agreements that, whenever a female was found, they would be allowed to see if she was one of their pack's mates first.

However, this rule was followed less and less because things increasingly became worse.

Around 50 years later, in the year 2134, the population issue finally became so bad that it was believed that the birth of a female baby had decreased by over three quarters worldwide since 2024.

Many more bloodlines had died out. Everyone was scattered at this point, living further and further from each other. Very few men had ever seen a woman, let alone found one to have a family with, so most men had become increasingly uncivilized. It was a "me vs them" world. There was an increasing number of men who no longer even saw women as the prized possession, their saviors, they had been viewed as in previous years. More and more women were not even being seen as human beings, but as simple breeders.

Though many human men and shifters did not agree with this way of thinking, in the new world they lived in, they knew they had to choose their battles carefully.

This was the year of the first Gathering.

CHAPTER ONE

Beep.
Beep.
Beep.

"Ladies and Gentlemen, please return to your seats and fasten your seat belts. As you can probably tell we have hit a lot of turbulence and may need to make an emergency landing," the pilot spoke over the intercom in a tense-sounding voice.

It's okay, just some turbulence, I thought to myself as I quickly made sure my seatbelt was on and tightened.

I gripped my seat's armrests as I looked around.

The flight attendants were practically yelling at people to buckle up while they ran to the back of the plane to buckle in themselves; not that anyone would have chosen this particular moment to act rebellious and not fasten their seatbelt.

But it was slightly disconcerting to see the flight attendants not behaving in the calm, collected, and professional way I had seen before in-person and in movies. If they were freaking out enough to be yelling and running towards the back, there *had* to be something more going on than just turbulence.

The plane suddenly jerked to the side, and my head slammed against the small window by my seat. I groaned, suddenly wishing I had not gotten the window seat. I could already feel the pounding in my head that would for sure lead to a killer headache.

Often when I had been on planes before, window seats were the seats I liked the best. But not this time.

Just my luck.

Blinking out the black spots and rubbing my head, I realized people were screaming, crying, and even praying all around me.

I didn't know what was happening. I had not been paying attention after I hit my head. But I obviously missed something. I mean, I'm not having a great time and just had my head bashed into a window. But as far as I could see, that was still simply a serious case of turbulence.

"Oh my God! We're all going to die," the person sitting next to me sobbed.

Looking over at the person who addressed herself earlier as Ruby, my eyes widened. Yep. I had to have missed something.

My voice came out as what sounded like a part squeak, part yell. "Why would you say something like that?! What's going on?!"

I grabbed the armrests tightly as the plane jerked again and the pilot voice came back on over the intercom. His voice was a garbled mess over all the noise of people screaming, crying, and the noises of the plane itself.

I could not make out his words. Turning, I looked out the window hoping to see I don't even know what. I couldn't see anything other than the dark shape of clouds, though. No one was telling me what was going on, the plane was now feeling like the worlds' worst wooden roller coaster ride, and I couldn't hear the pilot.

"Did you hear what he said? I couldn't hear anything. What's going on?" I tried to ask the girl next to me again.

Suddenly, a loud pop and bang rang through the air. Movement in the corner of my eye caught my attention fast enough for me to look out my tiny window again and see fire shoot from the wing of the plane.

The plane jerked to the side, tilting as everything seemed to fade into the background. I couldn't hear anything over the loud rushing in my ears. My head slammed into the window next to me again, and I vaguely managed to hear Ruby next to me say, "Ava, I think we are going to crash."

I did not reply because I did not want to voice the fact I was thinking so too. Then I heard another muffled shout that sounded like, "We're going down!" Which, quite frankly, was not what I needed to hear. It was seriously unnecessary commentary, considering my body was pushing against the seat belt at the sudden change in direction the plane was going; *down*.

Honestly, I can not remember anything else about what happened after the terrifying realization we were going to crash. All I could remember was the moment it dawned on me itself.

Then the night sky, which had been lit by fire in the previous seconds, was now black.

CHAPTER TWO

The world blinked in and out of focus. Then suddenly the darkness ceased to exist with a blind and penetrating light.

I groaned against the pounding in my head and blinked away the black spots from my vision. Sitting up with a hand to my head I looked next to me slowly. Ruby wasn't in her seat.

After carefully unbuckling my seatbelt, I slowly stood up. It was then that I heard groans, cries, and a little movement. As I moved to the center aisle, I looked up and realized the roof of the plane was gone. Wincing, I looked around only to gasp. There was blood and bodies everywhere. Some of these people I had spoken to earlier. I immediately started checking bodies for pulses. Then I heard a cry for help.

Looking up, I went towards the sound to find a bloody Ruby trying to help a guy who was barely hanging on. As in, the front half of the plane was separated and our half, which began at this guy's seat, was stuck in the trees. Relief filled me at the sight of her but quickly vanished when I realized she was about to fall. I quickly grabbed her and yanked her back.

"Ruby, you need to wait. We are going to have to think this

through because he has no floor and we have no way of catching him without falling ourselves."

We soon got the man down and found around forty other survivors on our half of the plane. It seems like a lot, but when you consider us being the better half of a plane that carries roughly 300 passengers, it's not.

After about 3 hours and a lot of teamwork, the people not seriously injured helped get everyone to the ground twenty feet below us.

A few men had gone to check on the other half of the plane but had only found three survivors and charred plane wreckage.

Since it was getting dark, we had all gathered around a fire that someone had managed to make.

Many of the people were injured badly, and we all hoped help was on its way. However, by morning we realized our best chances were to send out people who were mostly uninjured in every direction so we could try to find help. I happened to be one of them.

One of the men staying behind, who happened to be a doctor, said, "Now remember, there are 48 survivors. 28 female and 20 male, two of which are minors. 31 of them are in desperate need of medical attention. It is important to remember this because we need help as fast as possible and can't risk not getting enough help soon."

With the knowledge that so many people relied on the five of us, which included Ruby and me, we all set off in our separate ways.

It was close to sunset when I finally broke through the tree line and onto a dirt road. All I could think about was how thirsty I was- and how tired. Sitting down I decided to take a small break when I heard something in the distance. It sounded like a horse.

I scrambled up off of the ground as a horse-drawn carriage came around a bend in the road. I frowned wondering where we had crashed but pushed the thought away. It didn't matter. Help was here! I frantically began to wave my arms and began to walk towards them. I was too tired to do anything more.

When the carriage pulled to a stop I saw four men on it- and one other girl who had gone to search for help.

"Hi! Hi! I see you already have been told-" I began but the man stopped me with a gentle smile.

"Yes, we sure did. Don't worry we'll just make sure you are both taken safely into town and we'll get you all checked up."

I did not know why I had a strange feeling but shook it off. I was sure I was looking too much into his smile that seemed a little smarmy and his forceful response when I had tried to talk. So, I took the offered hand and got in the carriage.

I looked over at the other girl with a smile as I settled next to her and was about to talk to her; maybe introduce myself. But I stopped and my smile fell at the terrified look in her eyes and nearly imperceptible shake of her head.

What was going on?

We got into a run-down-looking town around 30 minutes later. I looked around at the ghost town. There was grass coming through most of the pavement. The buildings were empty, some with graffiti and broken windows.

Looking up from my place at the bottom of the carriage I asked, "Um where are we? Where is everyone?"

The same man who had spoken earlier didn't even bother to turn around to look at me when he said, "We are almost there. Don't worry."

We pulled up to a building that looked just as desolate and run-down as the rest of the town. It was huge, almost like a warehouse, and had candles lighting just the sides of the doors. My bad feeling was back and I shifted to stand up and ask something again when it happened. It all happened very fast.

I was suddenly grabbed, along with the other girl, and yanked off the buggy. Two men had yanked me out but two other men grabbed my legs when I managed to hook my leg around a part of the buggy as the girl next to me was screaming.

We were surrounded by men and there was nothing we could do to stop them. Then we were dragged into the warehouse-like building through a set of doors in the shadows.

Once inside I was thrown into a cage. At least that's what it looked like from the inside. I felt like a dog.

I quickly lunged to the opening but ended up grabbing the bars as the door was shut and locked before I could get through. I clung to the bars and started yelling, ignoring the sobs coming from the girl in the cage next to me.

I could barely make out the many men in the shadows but I knew they were there. Someone had to help us.

Though I did not know what was happening or where I was, I quickly came to understand that I was sure those men did not plan on helping us.

CHAPTER THREE

oud cheering rang through the darkness while I sat in what felt like dirt and hay.

I did not know how long I had been kept there. I was by myself in the dark, unable to see anything. The constant cheering in the air seemed to continuously get louder; which just seemed to make me more and more nervous and scared.

Suddenly light cut through the dark. The small globe grew brighter as it came closer, and I could see it was from a candle. The man holding the candle came into focus, and I saw he had two other men with him. Two men who were big and burly.

Scooting back into the cell a little more, I began to beg as they opened the door, "What is happening? Who are you and what are you doing?"

As they came in, they grabbed me and picked me up. Darkness blocked my view as something was pulled over my head.

Despite my struggle, I was taken away. I quickly began to panic and scream, "Help! Put me down! Help!"

After what felt like forever, I felt myself being slammed on something hard. Then I felt something rough being quickly wrapped around me, and what I was now sure to be a chair.

They were tying me to a chair! I began to struggle and tried to get away, but it was useless. The yells and cheers were now deafening. I thought to myself, *I must be in the room where I heard all this noise coming from.*

A man's voice cut through the loud noise in the room and said,"Quiet! Quiet everyone!"

The noise all at once ceased and a sliver of fear went through me as I listened blindly.

The same voice continued to say, "I want to welcome you all today for the 10th Annual Gathering here in Houston!"

I did not think it was possible, but the cheering sounded again and was even louder than before. However, just as soon as it started, it stopped.

The man's voice cut through the air again and what he said made me begin to panic even more.

"Now, I am sure you all know how this works, but in case you don't, I will go over it again. When we begin, the women will be revealed to you. Those who plan to bid will walk down, in a line, and decide which prize they want to bid on. Once they have decided, they will be taken to the assigned area in which they are to fight, either until one gives up or dies. Whoever wins, once making their payment, will be given escorts along with their woman. Then they can be on their way."

I heard myself whimper softly. They were going to auction me off! There were other women too! There would be fights to the death! Where am I? Who were these people?

The voice said, "If there are no questions, let the women be revealed!"

After a continuous cycle of roaring, there was nothing but silence for what seemed like hours. The thing over my head was pulled off and sudden needles of light blinded my eyes. Then my eyes quickly adjusted. I first saw a gigantic room lit by fire everywhere. The second thing I saw was that the room was full of men ranging from all ages and sizes- and they were all staring at the stage. At me.

I swallowed hard as I stared out at the room. I barely heard the announcer person saying,"-picked up in the middle of nowhere. No family and friends will think of her as missing. A feisty one too!"

I looked to the left and saw five other girls looking out at the crowd with fear, all of them crying. Some noisily, some silently. Some looked terrified, some confused, and some looking truly dejected.

I then looked to my right to see two girls in the same state, four girls with black bags over their head still, and one girl currently being 'revealed'.

I felt a gasp escape me when the bag was pulled off to show a crying girl who I quickly realized was the one with me on the carriage. The one who had also been sent from the plane.

Everything that was happening was pure insanity. Someone had to save us. How can stuff like this be happening and no one knows about it? Like the authorities! Where were they?

I can't be sold, be a slave, or possibly be killed. I was supposed to be on vacation!

I felt a tear fall from my face as I looked out at the crowd, but I quickly stopped crying. I could not show fear. I *would not* give these people the pleasure of seeing me cry. Whatever happened would happen and I would just need to find a way out of it.

I was quickly pulled from my thoughts, though, when I heard, "Let the bidding begin!"

I swallowed deeply and once again felt myself panicking.

Bidding?! Where the heck did we crash? Something like this did not happen in the U.S. and we had to be there. Right?!

I did not want to become another statistic. My breath started to come out in gasps, as I began to panic. I just hoped whoever 'bought' me would be nice enough to let me go. I internally gave an unamused huff. I didn't even believe that would happen.

CHAPTER FOUR

ours passed. I didn't know how many hours, but I was sure it had been many considering how many fights I sat there and witnessed. It was the only way I could try and somehow tell, considering how there was no way to tell time.

The sight of all of those fights had been horrible. No one seemed to care that we girls on the stage did not want to see what was happening below. It was very gory, with blood and skin everywhere. Snarls and even screams filled the air. It was horrible and even painful just to watch. Yet, there was one fight that particularly captured my attention, no matter how much it disturbed me.

Four men had stepped forward when they had called to those who would bid on me. The number of people bidding only on me was disturbing as it is. But the size and looks of three of them made me even more scared. Only one man, who was still muscular as far as I could tell in the shadows surrounding him- but not as much as the others, did not scare me like the others. He was the only one that I could see myself surviving with. I had no clue what the others would do to me- or even what he would do. Still, I did not see him doing horrible things to me.

Then they started to fight. The winners played against each other brutally. The men gave up only at the last second. Then, in the end, the one I saw only in the shadows and the man that I could only see from afar, was the one who 'won' me. This scared me even more because I had just thought he was the one I did not need to be scared of.

When it was all done the same voice as earlier, that came from a person I had yet to see, cut through the noise once more.

"Congratulations to all who have won their prizes. As explained earlier, please move to the hallway to make your payments. There you will be given a chance to freshen up and will have the opportunity to accept or decline the men provided to help escort your prize home. After that is all in order, you will be escorted to a private location to receive your prize so nothing shall provide any hardships."

I sat there in shock and fear thinking to myself, *This is really happening. I can't believe this is really happening.*

The voice continued, "Everyone else, please exit from the nearest exit and return home. I know it is a hard time, as of now, accepting your loss. However, keep in mind, there can always be another time. Thank you all for coming and goodbye."

Suddenly, something once again went over my head and I felt myself being lifted. This time, I didn't even bother trying to get free. There was no getting free when I was in a building full of lunatics who all were taking part in this cult-like activity. A cult is the only thing that made sense to me.

I do not know how long it was until the bag was removed from my head again, but during the time I had it on I was untied to the chair and just bound by my hands. Wherever they put me they seemed to not be worried I would attempt escaping.

When the bag was removed from my head I saw a small light coming towards me. I could not tell how far it was from me. As it grew closer and transformed into multiple lights held by many men, I became very scared.

One of the men did not speak to me but handed his candle

off and lifted me to my feet. Gripping the rope that was holding my wrists together he began to untie it.

Against my better judgment I asked, "Who are you? What are you going to do to me? Why are you untying me if I can just run?"

Immediately I mentally pinched myself. *Why did I feel the need to ask those questions? Especially the last one. Maybe I could have escaped if I hadn't.*

Then I looked around at the few men I could see and realized none of these men were the person who won me in the fight. Maybe these people were here to rescue me!

That thought was quickly squashed when I saw a new light separate from the others and heading our way from a different direction.

When this man got closer my breath caught. Not only because this newcomer was the person who bought me, which means these men were not here to rescue me, but also because of how ruggedly handsome the man was.

He was bigger than I had realized. Even with the candles, it was still very dark. But I could see enough to know I was very wrong assuming he was the smallest and safest choice. His body was big but lean with muscle. Like honed strength that was lying underneath his skin, ready and waiting to be unleashed. But in a way that was entirely rugged and manly.

I must already be developing Stockholm Syndrome, I thought to myself. Why else would I be thinking of how handsome the man who bought me and will be doing who-knows-what to me is?

The man spoke then, in a voice that matched his good looks, "Do not fear. We will not harm you. Ever. As to your questions you asked- you are going to come home with us, with me, of course. I can tell you are smart enough to know running would be useless and you would essentially get nowhere other than causing us to have to tie you back up. None of us want that. So, why shouldn't we untie you?"

I blinked. Fear filled me at the prospect of going home with these men. If I went home with them there was no telling how long it would take for people to find and save me. Let alone if I would ever be rescued. But I knew I could not escape from them here. As he said, I would get nowhere other than worse off if I tried.

The man continued, "As to who we are- my name is Leo Thorne. Everyone else you will meet later. But right now we must get going. It is already dark and if we are going to make it home in time, we must hurry. We already did not plan on stopping so we are behind. But we also don't want to run into any trouble on the way back. I promise all your questions will be answered in due time. For now, let's go."

Leo walked forward and grabbed my hand. When he did, what sounded light a growl emitted from him, scaring me. Not only was it scary, but what human being growls like some kind of animal?

Then he once again said, "Sorry. Remember, you have nothing to be scared about. I will never hurt you."

I let him hold my hand, telling myself it was not because it felt wonderful but because I could not stop him, and holding his hand was better than being tied up again. Then something else entirely hit me.

How did he hear what I had asked the other men when he was nowhere near close to us?

CHAPTER FIVE

I was not able to pay much attention to my surroundings at all because we were moving so fast. It was so dark, though, I'm sure I wouldn't have even seen things if we were crawling. These guys were creepy.

They were already creepy because of the whole cult thing, but they moved fast and seemed like they could see exactly where they were going- even in the pitch-black. Then there was also the fact the guy named Leo heard something I had said when he was nowhere near us.

I guess there were perfectly reasonable explanations for those things though. Maybe my words had echoed and I didn't realize it. Maybe their eyes just adjusted well in the dark. Maybe they were not going as fast as I realized and it just seemed that way. Still, it did not feel this simple to me.

Suddenly we began to slow down and I saw a lantern lit, the flickering of the flame growing in the dark. *Who still uses a lantern?* I thought to myself.

I heard the horse neighs right before I saw the cart, which looked like one of the old buggies on the Western channel. With a start, I realized these men also traveled like this. Not with cars, but with carts. I turned to ask why we were taking this and not a car when I realized there were considerably fewer men than before.

A thought occurred to me that maybe this was my chance to run. But then common sense kicked in. Even if I could escape, it still was likely they would find me right away.

The man who fought and bought me, Leo, faced me just then. I had not even realized we were still holding hands and was glad it was still pretty dark because I blushed. The last thing I needed was for my captor to see my blush and think I would lay down and accept whatever he planned to do to me.

Leo spoke in an attractive gruff voice, "We will travel in the buggy home. My men will travel with us but not in the buggy with us. You may not see them- but they are there. Do not worry, we will protect you. You will be safe on our travels home."

My eyes widened and I scoffed. I wanted to scream the thoughts rushing in my mind. *"Will I be safe? With the insane men who bought me like I was a calf for sale?! The only people who would harm me are you!"* I kept my mouth shut, though. The last thing I needed was to make him angry.

Leo helped me up into the buggy and came in after me. The lantern was brought inside with us and the door was shut behind him. He then turned and faced me while we sat side by side on the narrow bench.

My eyes widened and I blurted out before I could stop myself,"We are going to ride alone? What about everyone else? I didn't see any other...buggy's out there."

Leo watched me in a way that made me think of a cheetah before it catches its prey. Then a smile slowly began to spread across his face- which should have disturbed me but instead made my breath catch in my throat and my heart stutter.

His voice almost held a hint of amusement, but also was gentle, when he said, "Clearly there is no room for any others in here. Other than the two men up front driving the buggy, my men all are fine with walking. Besides, you are mine and I want to protect you and make you feel comfortable."

He set the lantern on a rack between us and looked at me again. I was not sure if it was the light from the lantern but he looked even more handsome now than earlier- and he had this look in his eyes that I would have mistaken for love if it made any sense.

He took both of my hands in his and a slight frown came upon his face, "You are freezing. Here, let me help."

He pulled me into his arms before a protest could come out of my open mouth, but I did not stop him. I was freezing and he was very warm. Besides, he also felt nice. I grew slightly irritated with myself at thinking that way about someone who had basically kidnapped me, but I couldn't help it.

I began to drift off to sleep, feeling warm and comfortable in his embrace, when he spoke once more- his voice quickly clearing away my drowsiness.

"I want to know everything about you, mine. I know you are beautiful and smart and strong just by what I have seen. But I cannot wait to make you mine and help you understand that you will never need to be worried about anything ever again because I will always protect you."

My eyes widened and I almost gasped. It was clear he thought I was asleep, otherwise, I doubt he would have said what he had just said. His words made me nervous and angry, though I also felt giddy for some reason.

I pushed aside the stupid and senseless happiness I felt at his words and focused on anger. My mouth opened to confront him and tell him what an insane freak he was but was interrupted by a sudden loud commotion outside that consisted of screams and bone-chilling howls.

Jumping in fright, my head shot up at the sound. Leo growled and faced me. He grabbed my head and said urgently, "Stay here, mine. They have come for you. My men are already fighting them off- but we will protect you. I am leaving now to help, but will be back." He then turned and jumped out of the buggy and shut the door behind him.

I quickly grabbed the lantern and jumped out, not thinking about the threat upon us. The way I saw it, they were either here to rescue me or a part of the sick cult and were going to take me. So I just needed to run.

Right then my eyes found Leo who had turned to face an attacker. I could see him clear as day and was grateful he had not spotted me yet. I turned to run, but before I could I saw something made out of nightmares that tore a scream from me. Leo had turned into a giant wolf right before my eyes.

At my scream, the wolf's huge head turned to me. It made sure I was okay- or not a threat more likely- and then faced its attacker.

I was going to run for sure then but somebody grabbed me from behind, lifting me completely off of the ground. I screamed again and started to struggle to get out of the person's arms. In my struggle, I saw many more wolves fighting men I had not seen before, so I assumed Leo's men were also wolves.

The person holding me yanked me behind a tree and a rancid breath, that smelt like it had eaten trash for years straight without being brushed, invaded my face. I fought off gagging. But it was the words that left his mouth that froze me in terror.

The dirty brute held me against the tree and said, "Listen, sweetheart, I will save you from the mutts but I will need my payment to be awful good. I've never had a woman before but I've heard the amazing things you can do. The best part? My employer will be so happy to have you, he won't care about me having a taste."

I could not help it, I started to cry. Cry was an underrated term; I started to sob. I banged my hands against his chest and tried to push him away but he was like a boulder, a disgusting boulder.

Then his weight was gone and I was faced with a wolf standing in between us, protecting me. His pitch-black fur was barely noticeable in the darkness of the night, but the darkness just seemed to amplify the bone-rattling snarl that tore from him as he faced the man. I didn't even flinch when the wolf- no, I knew it was Leo- ended the brute's life.

He turned back to me, saliva dripping from his jowls and blood pooling on the ground before me. The wolf's sides were heaving as he panted and his eyes slowly lifted to meet mine, glowing in the dark.

My breath caught because, at this moment, I couldn't care less that he had bought and kidnapped me or that he could turn into a wolf that just tore someone apart. Looking into the glowing golden eyes of the beast in front of me, the beast who protected me, I could not help but feel something inside me shift.

I was terrified still and consciously knew I probably could not trust him still. But a part of me knew my life was not going to be the same, and subconsciously I knew- though I was not aware of it at the time- this was where I was meant to be.

Then Leo, the human, was standing in front of me, pulling me into his chest, whispering words of comfort as I sobbed. After a while, Leo pulled back and brushed my hair back from my face. I could see him clearly thanks to the moonlight and he looked angry, terrified, and loving all at the same time.

Looking into my eyes, Leo started to talk, "Are you okay, Mine? I was so scared when I saw you being taken. I cannot believe I didn't get to you sooner. You should've stayed in the buggy like I told you- but I'm just glad you are okay."

He pulled me against him and I couldn't help but bury my face in his neck as I began to understand that maybe he was not really the worst person to be with.

Before I even realized it, a piece of the wall I built to not trust him fell and I whispered into his neck as I held onto him, "My name is Ava. Ava Kensington."

CHAPTER SIX

My body was rocking from side to side as the buggy began to move again. Leo held me in his arms, apparently taking the fact I gave him my name as a sign of something it wasn't. But right now I could not find it in me to care much after what happened. I was dirty; I felt dirty inside and out. My face had the stiff feeling you would get when your tears dried uncomfortably. I was also freezing.

When I got on the plane, I had dressed in light-weight clothes knowing I would get hot at some point. However, it also meant I was not clothed well to be riding in such cold weather.

I remember the bodiless voice at the place where I had been held captive saying something about Houston. I thought Texas was warmer than this, but maybe at night it was different.

Looking around I realized the cold weather and how dark it was outside guaranteed I would not run again. At least right now, after the horrible first attempt ended up. Besides, what if more men showed up again?

I really did not think I could trust Leo right now. I mean, could I trust someone who took part in something like buying another human being? But, whether I could trust him or not, I knew I was safer with him than on my own right now.

"You are very quiet. Are you okay?" His deep voice suddenly cut through the quiet space between us, effectively cutting off my thoughts and making me jump a little. "I am sorry, mine. I didn't mean to startle you."

Instead of answering his question, I wanted to ask him why he kept calling me 'mine' but figured he would probably not answer right now.

My voice came out shakier than I wanted it, "It's okay. I-I just am out of sorts and confused as to everything that has happened."

Part of me wanted to demand answers about what was happening. Part of me questioned whether he was as bad as I thought he was since he had done nothing but be nice and protect me.

I got sidetracked once more when I remembered what I had been trying to do before everything happened. My mind raced a million miles a minute, trying to sort through whether I should tell him. Whether I could trust him. At least enough for this. If they kidnapped the other girl and me, what was to say that they wouldn't do it to the others? A more logical, perhaps more sensible, part of me knew it wasn't smart to wait. *Some of them won't even be alive to have anything done if they don't get help fast.*

Also, there were men there. Maybe I could convince them to let us go help the other survivors, and the men would be able to save me.

My head immediately shook no, unaware of Leo watching me with both amusement and concern as I had my inner dialogue. These men could turn into wolves. Leo had fought men at that place and had fought the men who tried to take me. The men from the wreckage would not be able to do anything to help me.

Stop being so selfish. Whether you can be helped or not is irrelevant right now. They need help, and being alive and held captive with a chance to escape is better than being left to die slowly and painfully.

Ugh. I hated my inner-self sometimes for being so reasonable. I would not lose hope for someone to save me. I would not stop looking for opportunities to escape. But right now, there were over 40 people needing help and who were relying on me- if they had not been found already. As much I hated to say it, Leo was probably the only way I would be able to help them.

I looked up, barely able to make out his face in the little light provided by the lantern. His eyes kind of glowed a little but I shrugged it off.

I made up my mind and was going to say something to him, but I wanted some answers first.

"Leo?" A low growl tumbled through his chest at my voice and I jumped, unsure why he had growled or if he was upset at me. "It-it is okay for me to call you Leo, right?"

His eyes closed briefly as another rumble of his chest vibrated through his body into mine, but they quickly opened and found mine. His hand came up to gently brush against my cheek and I gulped at the tingles left behind in its wake. His deep voice rumbled an answer, "Yes, mine. Of course. I just like the sound of my name on your lips."

I blushed a little but decided to continue, "What are you going to do to me? What is that thing I was at? Why did you *buy* me? How is that even legal? Aren't the cops doing anything to stop it? Where are we? Where are we going? Why are we in a-a buggy and not a car or something? You are- you are a-a *werewolf*? Are you going to hurt me? Why do you call me 'mine'?"

I gasped and threw a hand to my mouth in shock and horror. I had not meant to blurt out all of my questions. I so hoped he did not get mad. Here I am trying to get some answers while not angering him and I got about it completely untactful.

To my shock and irritating delight, a deep rumble filled the air once more, only this time it was his laughter. When I continued to stare at him he stopped and looked at me with wide eyes. He asked, "Wait. You're being serious? You do not know what The Gathering is?"

Torn between angry and upset I shook my head no.

"Where are you from, mine?"

My brow furrowed in irritation, "I'm from a little bit of every-where but right now I am living in Alabama. I was on a plane heading towards South Africa when it crashed. But what does that have to do with anything?"

Multiple times through my answer his head had tilted in a way that reminded me of a dog- *or wolf.* His eyes were filled with confusion.

"Why are you looking at me like that? Why haven't you answered any of my questions? I feel like I have the right to know." I crossed my arms, sitting back and putting some distance between us.

"What time are you from, mine?" He asked.

"What time? What do you mean what time? It's 2019." I was beginning to get irritated. But something held me back from voicing so.

His eyes were wide as understanding, shock, and wonder-filled them. He turned to face the window, looking outside for a few minutes- silence filling the car. Just as I was about to say something, he turned to look back at me and gently uncrossed my arms so he could hold my hands. Then he spoke.

"Ava, I do not know how to say this. It is the year 2144. I-I have heard of this happening before, once around 50 years ago. There was a large vessel, I believe what you call a plane. It crashed one day, around the time my kind was just beginning to appear and things were beginning to become difficult. Some-thing happened, and I won't upset you with the details right now, but the plane came from the past. At a time where our world was beginning to need help with repopulation. See, more males are being born than females. It has gotten to the point where 10 years ago, The Gathering was created."

"See, there was a place needed to help...tame the violence of men fighting over and stealing women. We needed a way to repopulate the Earth, but we were still at the point where we did not want it to be repopulated where the same women birthed children from many different men. Also, many of us who were better off still had our morals and saw women as human beings, rather than just breeding vessels. Though I do not agree with The Gathering and how it is done, the mateless of my pack still go each year, hoping to find our mates. If we didn't, we could miss finding our true mate and having her go somewhere horrible."

I swallowed and stared at him in shock, not knowing how to process what he just told me or even whether to believe him. For some reason though, what came out of my mouth was, "Mate?"

Leo smiled gently and moved one of his hands to my cheek while his other hand went around my waist to bring me back to his body. "Ava, mine. You are my mate. My true mate. My 'other half' which was made just for me. You are mine. I will not and cannot harm you, nor would I want to. I will protect you, always."

I stared into his eyes, completely overwhelmed and not knowing what to do. The tingles and sparks running along my skin where he touched were not making matters any better. So, I once again blurted out the first thing that came to mind.

"My plane crashed and everyone is still there needing help!

CHAPTER SEVEN

A few hours later I was sitting on a log in front of a campfire. It seemed Leo, after hearing the fact there were more survivors from the past waiting to be rescued, had somehow called a halt to our journey. I do not know how, as he had not said anything aloud, but we had quickly stopped moving.

When I stepped out of the buggy with Leo's help, because it seems he is very protective of me no matter the circumstance, I saw men appearing around us in the dark.

Some of Leo's men got busy starting the campfire and carrying over a fallen log for me to sit on. No one spoke to me and no one came to sit near me once I sat down. Some seemed to stand guard around us and some were sitting on the ground on the other side of the fire.

As for Leo, he was standing a few feet away from me talking quietly to a man who was just as tall as him but slightly leaner. The man he was speaking to suddenly noticed I was watching them and met my eyes. A small, gentle smile graced his lips and said something to Leo while still looking at me.

Suddenly Leo turned towards me and came my way, with the man following.

Kneeling on the ground in front of me, Leo took my hands in his. He smiled and said, "Ava, this is Marcus. He is my Beta. This means he is like my second-in-command."

Marcus stepped forward and bowed a little, "Nice to meet you, Ava. I'd shake your hand but it seems my Alpha here has a bit of a possessive streak and is claiming you anyway he can." He laughed loudly and shook his head, "Don't worry, he's still an alright guy and knows he has nothing to worry about from me."

I stared at him with a slight smile, glancing from him to Leo and back. Marcus seemed much more approachable than Leo, and even though he was attractive- he still was not as attractive as Leo.

Licking my lips, since my throat was dry, I smiled at him and said, "It's nice to meet you too... um.. but if you don't mind me asking, what can I do for you?"

Both Marcus's and Leo's eyebrows rose and a smile graced their lips, but Marcus was the one that laughed once again. Marcus knelt also and responded, "What makes you think you can do anything for me?"

Feeling a bit more comfortable and confident around someone who seemed so normal, I laughed.

"No one here has spoken to me other than Leo and now you. So you must need something from me. And seeing as you were speaking to Leo right after I told him about my plane crash, I would bet it has something to do with that."

Marcus looked at me with wide eyes and then chuckled and glanced at Leo, "You have a very smart mate, Leo. You are lucky."

Leo grunted but smiled as he stared at me happily.

Marcus continued, " Well, Ava- May I call you Ava? It doesn't matter. I'll still do it, now. You told Leo that almost all the survivors are still there waiting to be rescued. I am wondering what you can tell us about them?"

At first, I was slightly irritated. He already found a nickname for me without caring whether I was okay with it or not. But a part of it was so normal and comforting that I realized I did not really care.

My brows furrowed and I pulled my hands from Leo's to cross my arms, "Well, if I remember correctly there are 48 people still there. Five of us went for help- three of us are female. I know another girl was caught with me a-and auctioned off. And- wait, wait, what does this have to do with anything? Are we going to help them?"

Marcus glanced at Leo and this time Leo spoke to me, "Ava, mine. Of course, we will help them. But we must know what we are walking into and how many people we may need to help. And, you must understand, though we will still help them, this is a world where there are way too many men compared to women. Many men have never even seen a woman, and it will be easier to find more men to help if they know there may be something in it for them."

He must have seen my eyes widen in horror as I was about to respond because he quickly shook his head and continued speaking.

"No-no, not like that. I have told you how you are my mate. You were quite literally made for me. There was no other woman I could be with, no other to compliment and be with me as you are. My kind, shifters, all have a true mate. But, in this world we live in, with so few females, many of us have gone without finding our mate. Lines have died off and some are even left to wonder if somewhere else around the world their mate is with another or has been kidnapped and auctioned off like at The Gathering."

He reached for my cheek, staring into my eyes as his eyes turned golden and he began to breathe heavily. I was not sure why or why I knew touching him would make it better, but I did. So, I reached up and placed my hand on the one of his that was on my cheek.

As he calmed down, Marcus decided to continue Leo's speech. "Ava, we only ever know our mate by being near her. It's all a mix of smelling her scent, looking into her eyes, touching her, and even simply being in her presence. So, we only ever find our mate when we basically meet her. But in this world, we may never find her, or we may and she could already be married with a family. Or she may have been through something terrible, like way too many females do these days, and cannot stand the idea of being with another. And none of us would force her. At least not here. So the idea that, like you, there may be more women who have come from the past that could be any one of our mates..."

Marcus seemed to close his eyes and take a deep breath. When he opened them, I could see something like longing fill his eyes, "Any one of us would fight to help another if it meant just one more of us would find happiness and be able to have a family."

My eyes softened at seeing his reaction. I glanced from him to Leo once more and then finally nodded, "I understand. Well, I'm sorry that I don't know ages or anything. Or how many are single or not. But, I am pretty sure I was told that 28 were female and 20 were male."

I heard gasps and glanced up to see all of the men staring at us from different areas of the camp they had set up.

I had not been paying attention but apparently, they had all been listening in to our conversation and agreed. But I was wondering why they all suddenly had such a reaction where they all drew my attention.

I glanced back at Leo and Marcus, seeing them also staring at me with wide eyes. "What's wrong?"

Shaking his head Marcus just fell back on his haunches as Leo finally moved to sit next to me on the log.

As I turned towards Leo, he wrapped his arms around me and smiled, "The second I smelled you, I knew my life was about to change. For the better. But I didn't realize just how much and that you would also help to change the lives of my men."

I frowned looking up at him as much as I could, while in his arms. "But... I don't understand, I told you they may not even be available or young enough."

Leo shook his head and laughed quietly, "Ava, you are mine. And you have given us so much hope simply because you said there are 28 females. That is such a large number that even if we find only one more of our mates there, it will be wonderful."

I blushed and looked down then suddenly looked back up, "There are also two children, by the way. We need to help them, soon. I don't know how long I've been gone and how far away we are. But there were significant injuries to many people. By the time we get to them, there may not be as many people alive."

Leo nodded and stood up, forcing me to stand up also because I was still in his arms.

Looking over I saw Marcus had quickly left and was talking to some men before they left, blending into the darkness and disappearing.

As Marcus started talking to more men, I saw some more men leave in a different direction and then I saw others start to gather everything. I looked over at Leo and asked, "Where is everyone going? What's going on?"

Looking down, he told me, "I am Alpha of this pack. But we are not the only pack. We are not even near our own territory. Our territory isn't even in Texas. So, some of my men were sent to the nearest pack of the location where you thought the plane was- based on the description you gave us. Some others were sent to the pack nearest to us to ask for some help and to send a message to our pack. We are beginning to get ready because once the pack members get back with some help, we will begin heading that way."

I was excited we would soon be going to help those who needed it but I was still both confused and a little wary.

"I don't know much about shifters... but I have read some books- enough to know that I would think it weird for other packs to offer their help."

Leo nodded, "Normally that would be true, but they also

have mates out there and they will be likely to help because they may find theirs."

I tilted my head a little as another thought occurred to me, "Leo, I doubt all of your men are here and I'm sure there are more that are unmated based on what you told me. So, what if one of their mates is at the crash and they aren't there to tell?"

He didn't respond immediately and when I looked up at him I saw him looking at me with something that looked like love and pride in his eyes. He also had a big smile on his face and I could not help but think to myself about how nice his smile was.

"You are already sounding like a Luna. You are perfect," he said while staring into my eyes.

"Luna?"

He chuckled and shook his head, "Luna is like the Alpha Female. It is what you are. Anyway, my men won't get here in time to help. But that is part of the reason why some of the men will be sending the pack a message. I hope, when we find your plane survivors, that we will be able to have all my unmated males look for their mate. Obviously, not everyone will find their mate. And the other packs we have spoken to will probably be doing the same thing. Soon, word will spread to other packs long and far, for them to also come to look- hopefully before the human men hear."

At his last statement, I felt my eyebrow raise in a silent question and he answered with a humorless chuckle, "It is one thing if a female chooses to be with a human male. But many human males, at least around here, have taken to having a more ruthless approach- such as The Gathering."

I nodded, remembering just hours ago having been tied up as men fought for me and one even bought me.

I opened my mouth to ask him something but a howl cut through the darkness that was beginning to lighten as it approached morning. Suddenly, more howls followed.

Leo stood in front of me, suddenly very tense.

I looked up, confused, as Marcus appeared next to us,

standing slightly past Leo but before me. *Weren't they the good guys?*

Noticing my confusion, Marcus grinned at me and gave a quick wink before saying, "Alpha males, mates, and other packs don't make the best mix, Ava."

My eyes widened in understanding as I blushed. I slowly reached forward and laid a hand on Leo's back and he relaxed a little- a real little.

Suddenly, I saw many wolves approach and appear in the dark. There seemed to be many that were tan-colored, unlike the black I recalled Leo being. One man suddenly walked from behind them. He must have stopped to change further back because I remembered, with a blush, that Leo had been naked when he had shifted earlier. I had just been too shaken to notice until later.

The new man stopped a few feet from us, seeming to stare right at me as I was peeking from behind Leo. Quickly he looked at Leo with a placating smile, as a growl tore through Leo when he had looked at me.

The man held up his hands, "Alpha Leo, I mean no disrespect. I just was amazed at how you have found your Luna and how she came to be here. Forgive me. I am Alpha Ethan. I am one of my pack's many mateless wolves. So, three-quarters of my mateless wolves and I will be traveling with you. But you do not need to worry about your Luna or her safety, from us or anyone else, as we are together. The rest of my mateless wolves will join us once my men here have a chance to see if they will be graced by the fortunate accident with their mate. If they have not, they will go to watch my pack and replace the others. As I am sure you are doing as well."

Leo gave a terse nod, "Yes I am, Alpha Ethan. I hope you are blessed as I am." He turned slightly so I could be more visible but didn't move, "This is my mate and Luna, Ava. As you can probably understand, my wolf will not allow you to meet her any more than that."

The other Alpha, Ethan, seemed to have a slight smirk but nodded, "Of course. Now, if you are all ready. We should be going before the sun comes up. It will be getting hot soon and we will want to be there before the sun is at its peak."

Leo nodded and looked at Marcus. They didn't say anything for a few seconds but then Marcus nodded and left, which I thought was weird. But I shrugged it off as Leo grabbed my hand and brought me back to the buggy.

We climbed in and Leo, once more, grabbed me and brought me to his side. This time he was tense, though.

Then we began to move and I could not help but smile. I was not sure what the future had in store for me or whether I could trust Leo fully. I did not know if I would be able to get over how we had met- though if I was being honest I was already starting to slow. But I knew I was making progress because we were going back to help the others.

I just hoped everyone at the plane crash site, and the others who had been sent out to find help- especially Ruby and the girl who had also been auctioned off- were okay. Once I finished this mission, I would make sure everyone was okay. Even if I had to search for them. Even if I had to enlist the help of the man holding me to his body protectively.

But first, I needed to save everyone I could- everyone who had waited at the plane for five people they did not know to help them- and I would. Finally.

CHAPTER EIGHT

One thing that I did not think I will ever get used to is the fact we are traveling in a horse-pulled buggy. Which means going anywhere would take forever.

It had been hours since we turned around to head to the pack nearest to the plane crash. I did not realize how far I had traveled since I left the plane and was captured, and then my trip after with Leo.

I was sure, if I was not with them, they would be a lot faster. I mean, wolves ran faster than our current speed. But, as much as I agreed with that statement, I refused to be left behind.

I also needed to be there for everyone that was on the plane. I could barely wrap my own head around everything around me, and I had seen too much to think it was all a lie. But everyone who had stayed behind would not have seen anything to make them believe what had happened to us. Maybe that was wishful thinking.

Anyway, this wait was killing me. How could anyone get anything done around here? Since there were no phones, and it made no sense for a wolf to run back and forth between the place where we were headed, we did not know what we were walking into. Could they not call each other?

I looked over at Leo, "Are there no cell phones anymore? This wait is driving me insane!"

My question must have come unexpectedly because Leo's head snapped towards me fast, and he briefly looked startled. But that look quickly turned into confusion as he said one thing, "Cell phones?"

He looked and sounded so clueless that I knew he had no clue what I was talking about.

"You don't know what cell phones are? Phones? You know, things where you dial a number and hold it up to your face and talk to someone who is in a different place than you are? How do you guys communicate over long distances?!"

Some of his confusion seemed to have cleared up by now and he chuckled lightly, "Oh you mean our SATs. Yea, we have those still. We only have a couple back on our territory though. There is no point carrying one with us when we travel since we normally travel in our wolf forms. Can't carry it."

"SATs?"

He laughed now, "You know... our small devices that are connected to the things in the sky. Mainly humans use them now. But, since no one alive anymore really knows how to make them, the numbers have started to decrease. They will stop working and no one can fix it. So, now, many heads of the bigger civilizations or people of importance are the only ones who have them."

My eyes widened as I processed everything he just told me and then I said, "Oh! You mean, like you still have satellite phones? Okay. Well, I guess I understand why you wouldn't have it with you. It's just, I hate how long it takes to get everywhere without even being able to call anyone. I mean, we don't even know if they found the plane yet!"

Leo must have found my reaction hilarious because he started laughing again, which I did not appreciate. Frowning, I pulled away from him and crossed my arms in irritation.

Shaking his head, he grabbed me and brought me back to

him while saying, "I'm sorry, mine. I wasn't laughing at you. You were just adorable. And you must know, we don't normally take this long to travel. When we travel, we are also usually running. So, travel is not a very long thing."

I signed and begrudgingly nodded. I understood what he was saying. But I was not going to admit that to him.

Instead, I said, "It's okay. I am just so anxious. I'm not able to know if everyone is okay. If the others that left came back. If some people didn't make it. If the- the people you sent got there. If they are freaking out or grateful. I don't know anything!"

After my mini-rant, I breathed a little heavy and had a hand pulling my hair in frustration. Which Leo quickly remedied by gently taking my hand, untangling it from my hair, and then placing his other hand under my chin to force my eyes to his.

I met his eyes, and my breath caught. But, if you asked me I would not admit it. Part of me still does not know whether I could trust him. I mean, I believe he had proved to me so far that he would protect me. But that is my body.

At this point, it was my heart that I was not sure I could trust him with.

I knew everything was different here and we were mates. There were so many different things added to this equation that I knew my way of thinking had to adapt with it.

I also realized just because he bought me did not mean that I was his slave or anything. He did it to save my life. Otherwise, I would have gone to someone else- who probably would have made me a slave. I mean, he saved me and gave me something special I would have never had in my time.

I still could not help but feel that something was holding me back, though. But, right now, I was not feeling that.

Leo looked down at me with a smile and then he slowly leaned down towards me. I could feel his breath on my lips as he paused and whispered, "Ava... I'm going to kiss you now. Is that fine?"

My eyes were wide, glancing between his lips and his eyes.

His eyes were so blue. Almost like water that was so blue, it was like water one could see through.

I licked my dry lips as I glanced at his. They were so plump and he had a Cupid's bow. I loved Cupid's bows.

When I glanced back up to his eyes, they were now glowing gold as he stared at my lips and his voice came out husky, "Forget it. I need to kiss you now."

Then I felt my whole world shift.

As his lips touched mine I felt tingles and sparks, not just where we touched but across my whole body. I gasped and he took the opportunity to deepen our kiss.

It was nothing I had ever felt before and it ended almost as quickly as it began when the door to the buggy suddenly opened and Leo growled. I gasped, panting to catch my breath, as I pulled away to Marcus laughing.

In between laughing gasps, he said, "Hey Ava, can you breathe okay?"

He bent over, holding his sides as he kept laughing until a snarling Leo yanked him by the shirt and snarled, "Why have you bothered us?"

Quickly Marcus put up his hands and said, "Woah- Woah, boss. I was just coming to inform you and our Luna that we are coming up on the outer boundary of the pack."

Leo quickly let him go and any sign of what had just happened between us was gone. Which I was glad for because I did not know how to process it.

Leo quickly seemed to step back into Alpha mode, "Have their outer guards met us? We should wait until they escort us further into their territory."

Nodding, Marcus said, "Already on it, Alpha. They met us and suggested you two stay in the buggy with the Luna until we get to their pack's house. I think it's just because they have a human Luna as well and they don't want to inconvenience us."

Leo nodded and said, "Very well. I trust they would not do

anything with you and Alpha Ethan out there. But I trust you to protect your Luna at all costs."

Marcus seemed to bow his head slightly and said seriously, "Of course I will."

Then, when Marcus turned to shut the door again, Leo growled, "Oh, and Marcus... if you ever seem to barge in on us without knocking again... and laugh at my mate while she is gasping because I kissed her senseless- I'll collar and leash you. Literally."

Marcus laughed and I gasped, smacking Leo's shoulder while blushing. Then Marcus said a quick "Yes Alpha" and shut the door.

Facing Leo I was embarrassed and fuming, "Really? You had to say that?"

Leo, looking almost smug, shrugged and said, "It's true."

I blushed and faced away from him in embarrassment for the rest of the ride. But I couldn't help but replay the kiss in my head the entire time.

When I heard shouting and lots of noise outside I straightened and looked out the window. There were tent-like structures set up everywhere and people in clothes that I recognized. But there were even more people than from the plane.

I gasped and jumped out of the buggy, leaving a growling Leo to grab my hand and follow me. Glancing at him, I asked, "Why are there so many people?"

Leo glanced around in confusion and suddenly three men and a woman walked up to us.

Marcus suddenly appeared on the other side of me, while Ethan was on the other side of Leo with another man.

Leo was the first to speak, introducing him, then I and Marcus. Then Ethan introduced him and the man with him, someone called a Delta.

Finally, the man spoke to us, "Hello Alpha Leo, Luna Ava, Alpha Ethan... I am Alpha Gabriel and this is my Luna Ana, as well as my Beta and Delta. Welcome to my pack. Let us settle down inside and I will debrief you all."

The three of them walked away, with us following. Then we approached what looked like it used to be a plantation building. One of the ones that were beautiful but gigantic. But you could tell it was old, though well-maintained.

Gabriel spoke over his shoulder, "This is our pack house. We had so many people come, we could not possibly fit everyone in here. So, we basically made it off limits except for things like the restroom and infirmary. That's why you see all the makeshift living quarters around."

When we approached a room, Marcus quickly talked to some men I remembered from our wait by the bonfire, and Ethan's Delta did the same. The men looked like they stood guard outside as we went in. After everyone was seated, except Marcus and Ethan's Delta who were standing in the corner, Gabriel continued to talk as his Luna passed around drinks and snacks.

I smiled gratefully at her and practically inhaled the snack as Gabriel said, "So, apparently her plane was near the border of Old Louisiana. Which, as luck would have it, was significantly close to a territory. One of the plane's searchers must have encountered the territory because when we got there, many of the injured were being loaded up. They had yet to take anyone back to their land yet. So, after talking to them- and the girl hearing your name, Luna Ava- we managed to convince them to let us bring everyone here. However, they were insistent on coming as well. Which is why there are so many people outside."

Leo spoke up while holding my hand, "And where is their Alpha? I'd assume he would be here."

"Ah, well, you see, everything had happened so quickly and their alpha had not been at the crash. But they are coming here as we speak. The tents outside are for the survivors, their pack, and your packs. Right now, I am concerned with having space for everyone. Especially once word spreads to other packs. But, I hope that once each pack arrives and either finds their mate or does not, they will leave once rested. This is the only way to have space and, quite frankly, the only way to prevent any territorial disputes."

Leo nodded and said, "I thank you for your hospitality and help, Alpha Gabriel. I can assure you most of my pack will return to our territory once everyone has had a chance to check for their mate. However, as you can probably understand, I would like for my mate and I to stay with some protection until she is ready. These are essentially her people."

Gabriel nodded and then Alpha Ethan was also thanking him when the door barbed open and everyone flew up.

Ethan's Delta was suddenly in front of him, while Marcus jumped in front of Leo who was holding me behind him. On the other side of the table, was a much similar situation. At least until I peaked around and saw who it was.

Pushing around Leo I yelled, "Ruby!"

She squealed and ran to me, practically slamming into me while hugging me. If it had not been the hand steadying me on my back, from Leo, I may have fallen.

I hugged her back and said, "I was so worried about you! You will not believe what happened!"

While she simultaneously said, "Oh my god, werewolves are real! I was walking for so long, being eaten alive by mosquitoes, and came across a wolf who became a man! A hot, naked man! And then, at the plane crash, more of them showed up and they started mentioning you!"

I laughed and shook my head. As much as I was concerned for her, she seemed to have had better luck than I had.

I also remembered her personality was kind of intense in a 'way too happy' kind of way.

I smiled and stared at her, "We need to catch up so much! But first, I guess I need to introduce you to everyone!"

Which took a while and we had some issues when she gave a flirty smile to Leo, which caused me to get irritated. I never knew I was the jealous/possessive type, much to Leo's delight and Marcus's amusement.

But that was fine once she knew he was my mate and we knew that if she had a mate, he was not in this room. Poor Marcus. Poor Ethan.

Apparently, she knew everything I did about the shifters and mates. Maybe even more.

I smiled, as we all sat down with me holding Leo's hand. Everyone in the room seemed to be captivated by our stories as we told them to each other and caught up except for maybe Leo who was 50/50 considering half of my story was me being kidnapped and auctioned off.

But, as I looked around at the other men's faces, I knew our stories gave them hope. Hope for a mate, for a family, for a future. Maybe it was the slight romantic in me, but I was now starting to hope I could also help them.

When did I develop such a hero complex?

CHAPTER NINE

Our time in Alpha Gabriel's territory went by in a blur of chaos and confusion.

After Ruby and I had caught up in the office, the men decided to talk about some "pack business" and Luna Ana decided to bring us to their kitchen for some girl time.

I would have much preferred to have gone out to meet everyone who had come back from the plane crash, but all of the men had not wanted us to leave the pack-house without them. As it was, we were already being guarded by three men each.

They did not seem to think it was overkill considering we were still in the same house as they were. *Men.*

Ana made the three of us some food and we sat down to talk about everything from where we came from and what our world was like, to more in-depth tales of our travels after our arrival, to pack life. The last one was where I became more interested.

I had so many questions about this world, packs, and mates. But I also wanted some outside insight into my confusing feelings about this world and Leo. Preferably insight that was not from a man. Which made our current situation perfect.

Here I sat with two females, one that understood the world I came from and the other that understood the world I am now in.

It also did not hurt that we had spent probably an hour now getting to simply know each other. So, I felt comfortable enough to ask questions I have been thinking of.

"Ana, how did you and Gabriel meet?"

She froze with a cookie almost to her lips, which made me concerned that I had asked the wrong question.

"Oh- it's okay if you aren't comfortable-," I started but was cut off by her shaking her head and a gigantic smile spreading across her face.

She touched my hand, "No, of course not! I just- it has been so long since I was asked that question it just messed me up. But it was so amazing, I could never forget it. It almost feels like it was just yesterday."

I smiled a little at that and asked, "Wow, really? How long have y'all been together?"

Laughing, she had such a happy look on her face. Her eyes and face glowed with such a happy look. Ana was a person you could tell was completely in love with her mate.

"We've been together for three amazing years. You know what's funny? When we met, I ran from him! Can you believe it?" She cries out while laughing.

Smiling with wide eyes, Ruby asked, "Why? Because he's a shifter?"

For some reason, this made Ana laugh even louder. Tears were now starting to come to her eyes, "Actually no! I ran-," she paused and snorted- causing us to laugh. "I ran because he was wearing a cowboy hat!"

At this point, all three of us were laughing as she told us about how her mom told her stories about the Wild West and how cowboys were dangerous, dirty men.

"My mom would always tell me, 'Be lucky Ana, that you won't come across a cowboy here in Orlando, cause they'll tie you up to their horse, and force you to do their bidding'. I always thought she was crazy, but then again, I never had to worry about seeing a cowboy in Orlando! Then, I went swimming one day in this secret place I found, and I saw a man standing there with glowing eyes and a cowboy hat!"

She finally seemed to catch her breath as she sighed one of those love-struck kinds of sighs. She continued, "I knew he was a shifter immediately, and I knew his wolf was on the surface since his eyes were glowing. But all I could see was that stupid hat and hear my mom's voice in my head. But, I won't regret running because being caught was completely worth it. He chased me and when he caught me, he ended up marking me right then and there. At first, I was both terrified and ticked off. But, one look into his eyes- I knew. I knew he was the one for me. I had been captured by the cowboy- heart, body, and soul."

"What is marking?" I asked.

She looked at me startled and then chuckled, "Of course that's the part you would focus on. I keep forgetting you didn't know about shifters before. Marking is the first step of the mating process. So, basically, in human terms, it's the permanent engagement ring while the next step is the permanent wedding ring. Marking is your mate biting you on your neck- in its most simple form. It binds you together and creates the beginning of the solidified bond between you two. Once he bites you, he then licks over it- essentially ensuring you both transfer DNA so that everyone knows you're taken. But most people tend to do both steps at the same time."

I frowned but Ruby then asked, "Why? What's the other step?"

In the background, I saw some of the men guarding us shift uncomfortably. They almost looked embarrassed. *Interesting. I wonder why.*

Ana laughed and mischievously glanced at the men. She must have noticed how uncomfortable they were too. "Well...consummation is the second step. The reason why most people wait to do both at the same time is because they also have to mark us then also, and for shifters- when you mate- there... uh can't be...for it to work, well. Remember, it's... essentially, it's making sure as much DNA is shared between the two of you as possible. But also, I think part of it is to try to ensure the continuation of the bloodline as much as possible. Which these days, it makes sense. Most men are not lucky enough to even have a wife or mate, and we women- well we know how significant we are for the world. So no one is really complaining about the possibility of having a family. Besides, something happens during the second stage that we really can't explain."

"Let's just say, I have some attributes of a wolf I did not have before I was marked, like I have canines when I need them. It's really weird because I can't control them at all. The first popped up during our first time. It hurt so bad, but then I knew the only way to stop it from hurting was to mark Gabriel also. Now, we'll be together or I'll be super mad about something and they'll just pop out."

Ruby and I both sat there staring at her in shock and a mixture of horror.

My brain was processing everything and practically was thinking of Leo and me doing all of it. Would I be ready for that? Everything seemed to move much faster in this world. Which, to me, made sense. Even how Ana had spoken about having a family as soon as possible made sense to me.

That did not mean I was ready to go find Leo and get started, but it made sense. It did not make sense to Ruby though, who began to freak out. Which, I guess also makes sense.

Earlier, she had told us she just turned 18. It's crazy how a few years of age difference could change how you think of things. I mean, I'm just 21 but I feel so much older than her. Especially now.

I wanted to continue talking. I wanted to know more and ask them what I should do. More specifically, what I should do with Leo. With us.

But then the men walked in, Leo immediately coming to me and taking my hand, pulling me up into his arms. His face buried into my hair and breathed in. I wondered if he was smelling me or something.

That question was answered, though, when Gabriel walked over to Ana and buried his face into her neck. It was very obvious what he was doing and she seemed to like it. A lot.

Once they were, I don't know- satisfied- they pulled back and Leo spoke, "So, the doctor that was on your plane has been offered a job with the pack and accepted. He will be staying. Some men and two older women with injuries did not make it- but everyone else is now believed to make a full recovery. Apparently, Alpha Gabriel already explained to everyone what has been happening and mates and everything. He informed them, he will allow them to stay until they make a full recovery or decide where they want to go- or, if they so choose, will be allowed to be in the nearby village this pack helps protect. But, he also made it clear, for his hospitality, he required all the women to stay until all the wolves had a chance to search for their mate. He had to word it that way, and of course promise he wouldn't allow anyone to be forced into anything because some women got skittish."

Alpha Gabriel looked over at me sheepishly, "I'm sorry, Luna Ava. I would never allow them to be forced. They do have an opinion in the matter. But I also couldn't let them just leave when I have wolves who will be coming from everywhere to look for their mate here. Especially since we need as much help these days as possible."

I was not sure how I felt about it but I did understand why he did it.

Wow. What was happening to me? I sound like one of those people who do not get upset over anything. Which was not me.

Leo pulled my attention back to him and kissed my forehead, then whispered, "Come my little savior, let us go so see your survivors."

I blushed but quickly followed as we all left the pack-house and went to one of the biggest tents. As we walked, I noticed so many men watching us or staring towards the tent. I realized they all had a longing and hopeful look in their eyes.

Something sharp hit me in my chest as I thought about how many of these men would leave with that look of hope gone. Then I looked over at Leo and found him looking at me with the same look.

Imagining him with a heartbroken or hopeless look in his eyes hurt me so much more. I could not bear it if I was the one responsible for it. I always wished to find my soulmate and have a family. *And here he is,* I thought to myself.

I do not think I would be able to just jump in. But I now think, maybe I could trust him. At least a bit more.

Maybe I could try and see where this thing went.

With hope filling my own heart and the decision to at least try, I looked back up at him and smiled.

Two Days Later

"Ava!" I heard my name being called and I walked faster up the stairs into the Pack-house.

Don't get me wrong, I love how everyone has been so nice and welcoming to me. All of the humans from the plane crash see me as their savior and their sort of spokesperson to the shifters. All of the shifters treat me like I am a queen. Which is not as great as it seems.

If they think they have done something to upset or irritate me, they ask for punishment. If I ask for something they don't have, they get a panicked and scared look on their faces as they scramble around trying to do something to appease me. They even take it upon themselves to make sure I am never alone, looking at me like *I was* the mythical creature who crashed into their lives to personally save them.

I sort of understood it all. Like, I get Leo wanting some of his- I guess our- pack with me at all times. I mean, we are still on this strange territory of another pack with many different packs and men still visiting.

All of our single pack members had shown up early yesterday and half of them left early today, with Marcus leading them. So, at times, Leo was a bit overprotective. But really? Between the presidential-like position the humans seemed to have put me in, the almost angelic or royal position the shifters have put me in, and the fact I'm basically never alone... yeah, I kept walking.

What made it worse, though, was that I understood how I have come to change their lives and give them hope. But none of them really saw *me*. They saw what I had done, how I could help them, and who they wanted to see.

I sped up as I heard my name again, this time from another voice.

Due to the fact Leo is a visiting Alpha and I am one of the very rare Luna's of the world we had been gifted with one of the rooms in the Pack-house. For the time being, it was the only place I could escape to. Which meant, I just had to make it up the stairs and they couldn't get to me.

They were allowed inside to use the restrooms, kitchen, and some of the common areas. But they should know by now not to go upstairs.

You could work your way around 'getting lost' and going to the wrong place downstairs but not upstairs. They have all been here long enough to know by now- them having been here almost four days now.

Almost there, I thought to myself when I heard my name getting louder as I started up the stairs.

I'm childish, I know. But when you become an extroverted introvert who has basically not been left alone for 125 years, then come talk to me.

I am at my limit.

Yea, I may have been a recently graduated college student

who just wrote a bestseller novel. But that does not mean I liked people, socializing, or socializing with people.

College, for me, was not a big socializing scene. I had friends. Well, more like acquaintances I would sometimes hang out with. Many times they would try to get me to go out to the bars with them or go to fraternity parties. I tried. I really did. But those are not my scene.

Alcohol? *Tastes gross, is expensive, and is something you'd have to keep up with all night long while there was most likely no place to put it.*

Being sweaty and being pushed up against bodies- and usually having to pay for it? *Was that even sanitary?*

Food? *Nonexistent. Not that I would try any of it.*

Games? *Boring if there were any.*

Having to dress up to go out and be miserable? *I don't know why anyone enjoyed it.*

Standing up and/or walking for hours, most likely in heels? *It's so not worth the pain I'd already be feeling the next day.*

Music? *Well, that was about the only thing I enjoyed and most of the time it was either too loud or something I did not know.*

When I said I did not enjoy going out, I was not joking. As I said, I did try. I would go to some frat parties or the bars downtown. I would get dressed up and try to pretend I was anything other than miserable. But very quickly it became too much and I could no longer bother with it. Heck, who am I kidding? I didn't even last those times. I would get water, yes water, and go and sit down in some corner that I could find until I had any semblance of energy to find my friends. Then I would still end up leaving early.

When you were surrounded by people who place fun over school, and who would go out half the nights of the week, there was only so much compromising one could do.

I mean, why couldn't we just go to a movie or dinner? Clearly I did not fit into the world of partying and having fun that society dictated as college.

I would have much rather been at home by myself, watching a movie in pajamas. The fact I wrote a novel should be clue enough. Not only that, but I also wrote the novel under an alias. I valued my privacy and alone time.

Heck, the big trip I planned to travel around the world- which was the reason why I was on a plane- was even being done by myself. For the most part.

Oh no. It sounds like they are not stopping, I thought to myself as I cleared the top of the stairs. Leo and I's room was on the fourth floor. No way I could make it up there before they caught up.

Running down the hallway a little I just grabbed a random doorknob and ducked into a room, quietly shutting the door behind me. Panting against the door, I finally lifted my eyes to see the room and... I was in a closet.

Wow, just my luck.

I pulled away from the door, wondering to myself if the coast was clear when it flew open and shut faster than I could see what had happened or who had entered. But the sudden charge of the air around me and the raising of the hair on my arms and neck told me.

"Leo," I said in an attempt to sound irritated but it ended up coming out too breathlessly for my liking. "Were you the one calling me and chasing me? You could have told me instead of making me run and panic."

A low chuckle came from him through the darkness as warm, thick arms came around my waist and his head buried into my neck.

I shivered at the tingles from his proximity and touches, and the heat from his mouth on my neck. "No, Mine. I came looking for you after sensing your irritation and desperation, then saw the people vying for the attention of my little savior."

I huffed and crossed my arms between our bodies. The past couple of days he and I have gotten along much better. At least in private. We have both seemed to open up more to each other and become more comfortable with each other.

It probably helped that we were staying in the same room. Apparently, no one would even consider me being in a different room than him.

At first, I had planned on him sleeping on the ground but that did not even last two hours. I wasn't going to make him sleep on the ground when the bed was big. Besides, in his arms, I found the best sleep I had ever had.

Gosh. When did I become so cheesy? I shook my head to clear it and focus back on the conversation.

"I hate this. I don't mean to ignore them or anything, but they don't treat Ruby like this and technically she got help first! She'd be more than happy to talk to all of them. I just want to breathe without someone thanking me for saving their life or looking up and seeing I'm being watched by literal puppy-dog eyes across the room."

My body vibrated and I shivered again as a growl tore from his chest and Leo's head flew up, "Who was staring at you?"

Did he just snarl?

I shook my head and laughed in exasperation, "Oh hush. Everyone watches me and you know it. You also know it's harmless."

He grumbled, "It doesn't mean I have to like it. Especially if he's our pack. But I'll ignore it. For now. We should get out of this box and get going. I need to eat and tomorrow we are supposed to be welcoming the first of the international packs. So, we will be meeting with Gabriel either later tonight or early tomorrow."

Apparently, despite the drastic lack of modern resources and transportation, packs from around the world have been able to plan a trip here- and fast. No one has told me how exactly. But I plan on getting answers. Eventually. Tomorrow, though, we will be having our first packs from Mexico. In another three days we are supposed to be getting our first packs from Canada.

Yea, like I said. *Fast.*

Shaking my head I took his hand as we left the closet and

said, "Can we just get our food and take it to our room? I really meant what I said. I just want to have some privacy. We can go and watch a movie."

Yeah, you heard that right. The world is falling apart and so many modern amenities have become nonexistent. Even the important ones. But, leave it to men to find a way to keep things working like TVs and DVD players.

Leo looked over at me with a gentle look in his eyes and smiled lightly, "Of course, mine. No one means to upset or over-whelm you. But if that is what my mate wants then that is what my mate will get."

I rolled my eyes at his cheesy statement and mumbled some-thing about puppy-dog eyes, sweet talk, and annoying nicknames.

Arms quickly wrapped under my legs and swung me up into his arms as he huffed like a dog and said, "I heard that. Just like I heard you earlier. Don't call us that. We are NOT puppies or dogs." He spat the last words with disgust.

I laughed as I wrapped my arms around his neck to hold on, "Oh? And why exactly would I stop calling you that?"

He grinned mischievously down at me, "Well, I'd say I would make us stay down here for dinner if you didn't, but I already promised you we wouldn't. SO, how about, I'll think up another name to call you so I'm not always calling you mine. Even if you are mine. You'll have more than one name I can use inter-changeably."

I pretended to think about it and smiled a wide smile, "Deal."

We sealed it with a kiss that lit me on fire from within, seeming to start where our lips touched and spread.

I quickly pulled away when we walked into the room full of people, shifters and humans alike. They all started cheering or calling out jokes about us.

My head began to pound slightly as I made Leo sit me back down on the ground. I do not really understand how everyone could cram into the dining areas so much.

I stood there awkwardly as Leo walked away, not knowing what to do as I waited for the line at the food table to get smaller. I really did not want to talk to anyone.

But I did not need to worry because Leo, being the very thoughtful and kind man I was discovering him to be, had gone to skip the line and get us food. He had done this the past few nights, claiming it as his Alpha status. But right now, I was so grateful I did not argue.

I quickly took my plate from his hand and then grabbed his newly freed hand with mine, dragging him up the stairs to my reprieve.

"So, we have *Fast and the Furious*... all of them, *Braveheart, Gladiator, Terminator, The Purge*," I laughed and paused in reading through the movie selections.

We had just come to our room and Leo had already settled on the bed with our food. He had piled up our pillows against the wall and made us a sort-of fort-like structure.

But me? He had given me the job of choosing our movie from the DVDs this bedroom had and would not let me eat until I put one in. So awful.

"I have no clue why I'm surprised to find that the majority of the movies mankind decided to save and keep are action or horror. But I am."

A deep chuckle sounded from across the room, from where Leo was on the bed. "Well, we are men and wolves. I don't think it's much of a surprise. But, if it gets me some bonus points, when we finally get home, I'll show you our vast collection we've scrounged up from one hundred years of scavenging."

My brows lifted as a smirk flitted across my lips, "There are so many things you just said that I want-no, *need* to respond to and I have no clue where to begin. First, what does being a man and wolf have anything to do with your movie selections?"

Before I could blink, tingles erupted through my body as I was pressed against the wall, with his heavy arms on either side of my face and his body pressed up against mine.

His voice came out in a deep rumble, vibrating my chest. "It's because, baby, in the world you have come from I believe you call the ultimate man a man's man- and I am that but much more."

My eyes widened and my breath caught, leaving me suddenly feeling like I needed something to drink.

My tongue darted out to lick my suddenly parched feeling lips and I saw his eyes hone in on the movement, beginning to glow gold.

But, though I had decided to give us a shot and was beginning to develop feelings for him, I still had a part of me wanting to resemble some semblance of the control that I relatively had in my old life.

Though it did not come out completely as I had planned, I decided I couldn't delve into all that right now so I just decided to mess with him. "One, baby? Really? That the best you can come up with?"

Okay. Who was I kidding? I liked it. *A lot.*

"Two, a 'man's man?' Do you even know what that means, Leo?"

He growled, eyes still glowing but with a hint of amusement added to it, and leaned forward to nip the corner of my lip. Then he growled again without pulling away, his breath fanning over my lips.

"Of course I do, *baby*. It's a man who is comfortable in any environment. One who is strong and built- not from a gym or some set routine made to make him look appealing to a woman, but from hard labor and a hard-working life he chooses to live. A man who can take care of his woman in *all* the ways that count- whether it's keeping her safe mentally and physically or knowing when his woman needs a break. So he gets her some food and takes her to their room for a relaxing evening of eating and watching a movie- just the two of them."

As he continued to talk, my wide eyes stared in shock and wonder. Mostly because he seemed to be taking my personal definition of what a so-called 'man's man' was, but also because he was actually relating it to things he had done for me.

"A man's man is a real man who can take care of any situation you need him to but also knows not to hold you back. He knows, being a man's man, he has a woman who is just as strong-willed and wonderful as he is. A woman who will be there every step of the way with him as both *a* woman *and his* woman."

I swallowed, not knowing how to respond but I could practically feel my heart beating out of my chest.

Then he continued, "But like I said baby, I am not just a man's man. I'm more. Cause I'm also a wolf which makes me so much better. It makes it so you never have to worry about my loyalty or if I will grow tired of us. Cause I won't. I'll never stop thanking the stars in the sky for bringing you to me. And you'll never have to worry about my health and safety or what would happen if we were in a situation where I was protecting you against a whole army of men. I'd fight them until I died, our pack would fight them until they died. And Ava, mine, we rarely die."

"You'll never have to worry about our pups' safety or if I'll be able to love them enough or be a good enough father. Cause I will love them just as much as I love you. I'll make sure they are safe and provided for, just like you. I'll give all of you everything you ever wanted. But I'll also make sure they know to never take anything for granted, to work for what they need. I'll make sure they grow to be good people and grow to become surrounded by good people. I'll train them to protect themselves and protect others- to become the very best fighters around. Especially if we are blessed to have daughters. I'll train them to be leaders and to love- especially their mama."

He tucked a piece of my hair behind my ear and kissed me softly, "I'll love you, protect you, cherish you, give you everything you need and want that I can. If you need a hug or don't want to talk about something I'll know and I'll be there just to hold you. If I do something stupid like stay out too late working on Alpha stuff, tell me. Or not. I'll know how you feel and spend the whole next day with you in my arms. You are *mine*, Ava. And I am yours. Always and forever."

"I am a man and a wolf. I can be rough around the edges sometimes. I have slept and will sleep out in the woods. I chop wood and shovel snow- sometimes with my paws. I am an Alpha. I'll get protective and possessive. I'll get jealous and irri- tated. I'll get stressed out and silent. I'll get angry and busy. I may have to leave for days or weeks at a time- which most likely I will probably drag you with me. I'll get clingy and...*hungry*."

"I *am* a man and I *am* an animal. I love carnage and fights. I love running fast and being out in nature. We live in a 'wolf eat wolf' world out here where I won't hesitate to destroy someone if I have to. But I will always love you. Always come back to you. You may need to hold me or talk to me. Sometimes, maybe even boss me around or let me run it off. Sometimes, you'll just need to try and understand what I'm doing and let us talk about it privately later that night. Just always be there for me and I will be there for you. Together. Mates first, parents second when the time comes, and leaders third."

His lips took mine, fully this time, not letting go until I thought I would pass out from lack of oxygen. Which didn't really help me feel any less stunned and dizzy than I was feeling from his speech.

"So, baby, yes. I do know what a man's man is and that is why action movies and horror movies are mainly around here. We do have *a lot* of those at home, but our pack's ancestors also did as much as they could to both preserve what they could of the old world while also prepare for the hope that one day the world- or at least the pack- would not be so drastically unbal- anced between men and women."

I was panting from our kiss and still unable to process anything, at least to be able to say anything without it showing just how much his speech had impacted me. So, I said the first thing that came to mind.

"Um...I don't think I've ever heard you say so much in one sitting before," I said in a squeaky-sounding voice.

He growled, but when I looked up at his face he was smiling so I knew he was amused and not upset when he said, "Really? After all that, that is all you have to say? Anything else?"

Turning my head, looking towards where the DVDs were, I croaked out, "Um yeah, let's just watch *Fast and Furious.*"

Without looking at him, I pulled away and put in the movie.

"I sure do hope you guys have the *Fast and Furious* series in your pack also, otherwise we may need to end our time here by...liberating them of theirs," I said innocently.

Then I took his hand and led him to the bed, not giving him a chance to respond by making the movie start. Once settled onto our current fort-like bed we watched the movie, ate cold food, and then held each other. Together. In complete silence. But not uncomfortable.

A man that was more than a man's man and his woman.

Almost the entire length of the movie later my breath caught as I realized what he had said earlier.

I love you.

I did not want to think about how that made me almost feel sick. Sick in a 'butterflies in my stomach' kind of way, not a grossed out or terrified kind of way.

Though I was terrified of how happy I felt about him feeling that way. I knew I cared for him and my feelings were growing more each day. But love? We had really just met. Yes, we were getting to know each other every day. But I was also getting to know, well, everything. It was way too soon for love.

Wasn't it?

CHAPTER TEN

Opening my eyes to the bright sun filtering in through the window, three things immediately came to mind. The very first thought was how bright it was without the use of curtains. The second was remembering last night and how amazing it was. Just eating in bed, watching a movie marathon, and in the arms of the man who is apparently your soulmate. Though, I could *not* think of what he said. I just was not ready yet. The third thing that came to mind was how warm it was under the thick arm holding me to him.

Wiggling a little, trying to move, I succeeded in turning just enough to be on my back so I could stare at him. Not exactly what I had in mind, but not necessarily a bad outcome either. I chuckled to myself.

Staring at him in his sleep was something so completely different than while he was awake. Leo could not be considered boyish, even relaxed like he was while sleeping. But the rugged lines of his face were just enough relaxed that it felt like I was seeing a piece of him only I got to see. Smiling, I raised a hand to his face but stopped just short of touching him. I did not want to wake him but my eyes wandered all over his face, staring at how the light played over his features.

When I looked up I was startled to find glowing eyes smiling at me.

We had progressed in our relationship so much. At least in the area of being comfortable with each other.

We kissed some and held each other in our sleep. We talked often and about things that meant a lot to us.

I was still unsure of what any of it meant for us or how I was supposed to proceed in our relationship. But I hoped to soon get some more one-on-one talks with Ana.

I felt she was the only one I could talk to about this situation.

Ruby might be of some help but I still felt like she would not fully understand what I was going through.

I knew I was beginning to feel romantic feelings for Leo. But I could not figure out if they were just forming because of the situation we were in. The fact he saved me, was apparently my soulmate, and the fact we kissed sometimes and slept in the same bed. Or if that was just our story and I was beginning to fall for him.

But I could not make myself take any "next step" until I figured out this internal battle I was having.

Even though I knew he wanted to move our relationship along based on his eyes. I have learned when his eyes glow it means he's feeling some strong emotions like anger or desire.

Shaking away my thoughts I smiled at him and said softly, "Didn't know you were awake. Did I wake you?"

He chuckled softly and shook his head no.

I finally touched his face, following the line of his jaw, and said, "You should've told me."

His voice sounded even gruffer from sleep as he said, "Then I wouldn't have had such a wonderful wake-up call."

I blushed and glanced down but then felt my face tilted up. Then he kissed me gently.

He pulled me towards him, rested his forehead against mine, and whispered, "I can't wait until we are home and I can just stay in bed with you all day instead of constantly having to handle pack business."

Still blushing, my eyes widened, "Awfully presumptuous."

He chuckled and shook his head a little, "Not like that. I mean sleeping in, talking, watching movies...or that when the time is right. But here, my guard is never down and we are surrounded by many other packs. Many other men. And we have to constantly be present. No staying in our room or pushing back on our responsibilities."

I smiled, "I know. I know what you meant. And you already know I feel the same way. Otherwise, we would have eaten downstairs last night."

I pointed my toes and my back arched, some cracking noises seeming so loud to me as I stretched a little.

"But, even back in my time, we would always have to force ourselves out of bed to get the things done we needed to do. Even though we definitely didn't want to."

As I slipped out of bed and pulled the sheets on my side up I smiled as he said, "We're not that different after all."

"I for sure would not say that. We have air conditioning, for one. At least where I lived. I wasn't sure if I'd be able to fall asleep last night with how hot it was. And this morning, being woken up by such a bright light that I normally would have curtains pulled so tight a sliver of light would be too much for me."

I turned away and walked to the few articles of clothing I had been offered, and figured out what I would be wearing.

"Also, we had so many different options if we didn't want to get out of bed. We have this thing called Netflix where we could watch movie series and multiple movies over and over all day long. We could order food and have it delivered straight to our door. Where we never have to leave or cook. We could play games when we wanted; listen to music and dance if we wanted to move around. And worry about the next day and stuff we had to do later."

Leo was still in bed with his hands interlocked behind his head, watching me as I talked.

I turned around while holding my clothes in my arms as I smiled at him. "A little the same but a lot different. I'll change now. You should start getting ready too. Today's not one of those days we can just ignore the world."

I turned and went into what used to be a working bathroom. It still worked, mostly. But, water was limited and so was electricity.

I honestly hadn't figured out yet how exactly they had electricity here, albeit a little. But I had figured out the water part. A part of it at least. It was kind of hard to miss the two big faded blue jugs on the top of the buildings which were water catchment devices. Which could mean, if you got a lot of rain you were set on water for a week or two. If you didn't get rain, you didn't have water. I don't know if they have a well or something else to balance it out, but probably not seeing as how they were shifters and most of the water they needed was for their Luna's convenience. Everyone else was probably perfectly content going down to a river or stream or whatever it was. I hadn't had the chance to see it yet, so I didn't know which it was.

Anyway, you just had to pay attention to what you were doing and not go overboard with the electricity or water. What water you had that day may be the last time you have water for weeks.

After using the restroom and washing up a little I changed and came back out to see the bed made up and a shirtless Leo about to finish getting dressed.

I blushed and looked down then back up to his chuckle and him saying, "Ava, mine. Looking at me is nothing to be embarrassed about; especially liking it. We are mates."

Once he was done, he walked over to me and took my hand.

"You look beautiful, baby. You ready to get going?"

I was constantly blushing around him and it was starting to irritate me, but I couldn't help it.

So I looked away and said, "Yep, let's go. I'm seriously craving some tacos and the sooner the Mexico packs get here, the sooner I can figure out if my Mexican food days are behind me or if there's hope."

Now that I thought of it, I was starting to get anxious about what ingredients the world still had and what I meant for my normal diet.

My diet was so centered around Mexican, Italian, and Southern food- really all things restaurant and fast food- that I really was nervous about going through withdrawal.

It may seem so trivial, but if I had known the last time I had queso and chips was the last time, I would have eaten a lot more than I did. I also would have probably tried a bit harder to learn how to cook if I had known I would soon be in the future with a drastically smaller population and no delivery or Drive-Thru.

Leo chuckled under his breath and shook his head as we walked hand-in-hand out the bedroom door and down the stairs to begin our day. He thought I was joking or exaggerating.

Until he experienced Taco Tuesday, he wouldn't know.

As soon as I could learn if they were even still a possibility, then I could figure out how to cook them. Then, once we headed to Leo's pack, I would make it into a normal thing. Leo's pack will never be the same if it worked out. We would have Taco Tuesday as much as possible. Once they tasted it, they would beg for it.

Until then, werewolves just don't understand.

After we got downstairs, Leo kissed me on my forehead and left me in the kitchen. He was going to find the others, to figure out just how far the first of the Mexican packs were from getting here.

I felt *giddy*.

There was no other excuse for the truly gigantic smile which spread across my face as I remembered our night last night.

It was perhaps the closest time I had gotten, so far, to having a day that was "normal"; and I had gotten to see a much different side to Leo. It is crazy just how far we were moving along in our relationship. I mean, I really didn't care about the fact he's a werewolf and basically over a century younger than I was.

Wait, what?? Don't think about that, Ava! Don't go there. Nope, no, nada. You don't look a day over 21. I shook my head at my internal monologue and laughed aloud.

I didn't even really care how we met anymore, either. But part of me still didn't like how fast I was settling in. Then again, there was not another option. When life changes, you have to change with it at some point or it will leave you behind.

I mean, what other choice did I have? Run off into an unknown world, abandoning the man who was apparently made for me, and probably getting kidnapped again while I was at it? Build a plane by myself somehow, learn how to make jet fuel, learn how to fly a plane, and hope I survive the crash which may or may not even take me back to my time? That was just stupid thinking.

This was my life now and it didn't seem like a bad one.

I walked over and grabbed an apple from a basket on the counter to eat as my breakfast. Then I turned around and I jumped in shock.

Ruby was standing in the kitchen doorway with crossed arms and narrowed eyes.

For some reason I shifted uncomfortably, not knowing what was going on but feeling a rush of foreboding.

CHAPTER ELEVEN

"Ruby! Oh my gosh, you scared me," I gave a nervous laugh, "I didn't hear you come in. What's wrong?"

I must not have heard her come in while I was lost in my thoughts. But now that I'm seeing her, I was getting a vibe that I didn't quite know how to read.

Normally Ruby was so easygoing that I was concerned about whatever had rankled her enough for me to be able to tell she was irritated.

A thought crossed my mind real fast and my eyes widened as I took a couple of steps towards her. "Are you okay? You haven't had any issues with anyone since we last talked, have you?"

Ruby shook her head, "No... I just don't understand how you're already sitting back and relaxing when we are *in the freaking future being held captive by werewolves*!"

Towards the end, her voice had raised and she was throwing her hands around.

I was so shocked at her outburst, but more so at what she was actually saying, that I took a step back.

I felt like I had to pick my jaw off the floor before I could respond, "What are you talking about, Ruby? Where is this coming from? You haven't had any issues with this before that you've mentioned. And it's not like we can go back in time. Besides, you know that's not true. We aren't being held captive. They saved us!"

Ruby was already shaking her head, "How can you say that? You of all people?! You should know! Leo bought you from a dang human trafficking ring and now you're kissing him and sleeping with him and- and basically jumping into a Disney love song number every time he leaves you and you think no one's around to see! And now here we are, just taking their word for everything as we wait to be married off to more of their kind! How do we even know for sure what they're telling us is true?!"

My eyes felt like they were about to pop out of my head and I felt very conscious of the fact many ears were most likely hearing us speak right now. But I also could not figure out where all this was coming from, from her.

I felt like that was very important for me to know where it was coming from to know how to proceed. Because if she was really believing this, after everything we had seen and heard, nothing I could say would make it better. But if she was just stressed out and breaking down, well I could try and be there for her until she calmed down. But I really didn't know how to respond, no matter what.

"Ruby, you don't understand what you're saying. You *know* that isn't true. And quite frankly, you're one of the closest people I have to a friend here, and I will love to chat with you about anything- but when it comes down to it, what happens between Leo and I is none of your business!"

Her mouth dropped as she stared at me and I thought maybe something I had said had gotten through to her until she narrowed her eyes again.

I could practically see the fire in her eyes and was not in the mood for one of the epic teenage rebel-type rants I was sure she was about to do.

Gosh, *I am so* old *now.*

So, I decided to keep talking before she could.

"As for all of the other stuff, you know they aren't lying to us. As you said, I know more than anyone. I've *seen* more of what's to see of this new world we are in than anyone- including you. It's not a lie. And I can agree, it's not the best of circumstances. When I found out, I was not happy. About any of it! But I also understand. This new world we are in is one *very*different from what we came from. And it sucks! It's horrible and unfair, but it's what we have now!"

I had begun to pace back and forth now while staring at her.

"It's our world now, Ruby. There is no going back. Any hoping and wishing is only going to make you miserable. So don't! We aren't being forced into anything here. The least we can do for all that these people have done for us is to stay in one place while they try and see if something comes out of some-thing that was decided before we were even born. You may not even have a mate! But even if you do, you have a choice! If you leave, I can promise you it is very different! You think *this* is being held captive?! You were right earlier. *I know* what being held captive is. It's definitely not this!"

I paused to catch my breath and I became painfully aware of how quiet it had gotten.

I looked behind Ruby to see several people staring at us with wide eyes, one being Leo. I met his eyes over her shoulder and everything in me relaxed as I saw his anxiousness but also pride. As I caught my breath, I looked back to Ruby and this time spoke in a softer voice.

"I know it's scary. All of this is completely unknown. For all of us. Even me. But all we can do is take it one step at a time, one day at a time. If you need to vent or rant or cry or laugh we are all here for you. Everyone from that plane is in the same boat as us, Ruby. But getting upset and freaking out and lying to your-self to try and make sense of things is not the way to feel better."

"I'm not saying you have to be happy about this stuff and just take the hand we've been dealt and move on. But if you get stuck in the past and don't try and find a way to be happy here- if we all don't try and find a way to be happy here- then we won't ever be happy. We won't be living and we might as well have never gone out looking for help after our crash."

I walked to her and gently put my hand on her shoulder as she stared at me with tear-filled eyes.

Leo smiled and tilted his head to get my attention, then mouthed that they were here.

I gently smiled and looked back at Ruby, "I'm here if you need to talk. But for now, go cool off and do whatever you need to do. I know it's not the best situation, but now we do what we need to do to survive. To live."

I rubbed her shoulder a little before letting go, "One of the Mexican packs is here. Take your time before coming out. We'll be there if you need us."

Then I went over to Leo, took the hand he offered and buried my face in his chest as he walked me out so I wouldn't have to look at the others who had witnessed what had happened in the kitchen.

I hope none of them took it personally but I was kind of wrecked by the giant roller coaster ride I felt like I had ridden emotionally.

For a day that had started so great, I sure had experienced so many different emotions already. I just hope it gets better before it is over.

I looked up as Leo smiled at me, "I see you never got to eat your apple with all your Luna duties going on."

"Luna duties," I asked in a voice which came out as a squeak, "nope, no Luna duties... just dealing with a mental breakdown that almost led to a mental breakdown of my own."

Leo chuckled and kissed my head, " It's okay, mine. I'll find us somewhere where you can eat something after the initial Pack introductions. We won't be doing the meet and greet for everyone to see if they have their mates until later. Hoping to do it when one of the other packs gets here tonight. Two at once. Besides, I have my Luna already. You're the one I need to make sure is cared for."

He smiled at me cheekily at the last bit and I blushed but shook my head. I was still overwhelmed by what had happened in the kitchen.

At this rate, I think only two things could make the day better again. Seeing as I didn't think Leo and I would be able to hide out in our room again tonight, the only other option to save this day would be a certain meal for dinner.

I sure did hope they would help us out with dinner. Maybe make some enchiladas and tamales. A whole Mexican buffet would be awesome. I don't think we would be as lucky to get Queso and chips, but a girl could dream.

But there was one thing that would definitely make it all better. *Tacos.* I needed some tacos. Tacos and pizza were always my comfort food. I did not see myself having pizza any time soon. But tacos- well I'd at least know after today.

We walked outside of the main house and I squinted against the sun. I would never get used to waking up so early. But I guess I'd have to learn to try my best.

After what had just happened in the kitchen, the aspect of me suddenly having to wake up early for the rest of my life was just the cherry on top of an awful sundae.

Once my eyes adjusted I looked around. I could tell there were more people than normal. More wolves than normal. But they all looked hard for me to tell apart still.

However, several men were standing and talking to Alpha Gabriel, Ana, and a bunch of other pack leaders. I could tell immediately they were our first Mexican visitors and I felt a smile grace my face.

If I wasn't in public I probably would have been doing a happy dance. *Tacos here I come!*

A chuckle escaped and Leo looked over at me with a raised eyebrow.

I just grinned and whispered, "Taco Tuesday!"

I suddenly heard a laugh and looked over with wide eyes, remembering the fact I was surrounded by men with insane hearing.

CHAPTER TWELVE

I groaned and shoved my head in Leo's arm to hide my burning cheeks as more chuckles joined the one.

I heard some Spanish words and then Leo pulled me forward. My body shook a little from the rumble of his voice as he introduced us, "Hello, you must be the Sonora Pack. I am Alpha Leo and this is my mate, Luna-"

"Ava, sí. We know all about Ava. The Luna who has given us a light in the sky. Encantado de conocerla, Luna Ava. I am Alpha Silverio and aquí es my Beta Teo. You can call me Silver, señora."

He reached over and kissed my hand, but quickly let go at the sounds of Leo's growl.

"Hola Silver. Hola Beta Teo. Cómo están? It's nice to meet you," I responded with a small smile. Still embarrassed about my earlier comment.

He chuckled a little and winked at me before saying, "Oh! Bueno! Tu hablas español? Y what is this about tacos? Is our lovely Luna experienced in Mexico? Te gusta la comida mexicana?"

Leo's arm wrapped around me and pulled me up against his side. With a raised eyebrow I looked up at him to see him staring at Silver with slightly narrowed eyes.

I chuckled at Leo for being jealous of Silver. I mean, I may love tacos but come on. I wasn't going to leave Leo for someone who can cook them. Maybe.

I smiled as I glanced back over at the Mexican alpha and said, "Solo un poco. Estoy muy...oxidado. Pero sí. Tengo hambre de comida mexicana. Lo extraño tanto. I was hoping making things like tacos and enchiladas was still an option and you may be able to teach me while you are here."

I blushed a little. *Way to not jump right to the point.*

"If you can, of course," I shake my head, "I know that is not quite your priority here."

Everyone chuckled and Silver said, "Of course! We were making our food long before those modern conveniences you are used to, and we are still now. As luck will have it, I pride myself on my ability in la cocina. So I would love to help you learn. If we have time."

Leo's hand tightened on my waist and I looked up, "Leo, you will just have to be there and learn to cook with me. You know, so your jealousy can maybe catch a break."

A growl filled the air as others chucked and Leo looked down at me, "I am not jealous. I just know what is mine and when others should be aware of that. But if this is a definite thing then maybe I will be joining you for these taco lessons you keep on about. Can't have my Luna doing all the cooking, can I?"

I blushed but grinned.

Looking over at Silver, I was ecstatic and said, "That sounds great! Maybe we can have a taco night tomorrow if we find time today for you to teach me and we can find enough ingredients!"

He nodded, "That sounds lovely. A wonderful chance to have a celebration feast for hopefully many new mated pairs. If we can find enough of the ingredients here for all of us, then I shall make time today for our lesson."

Ana finally spoke up. I had forgotten she was there until she did so, but she smiled and said, "I'd love to join as well. Gabriel and I will have some of our pack go on a run to see about the ingredients if you give us a list of what we will need."

Alpha Gabriel nodded and nuzzled her head before saying, "Yes indeed. Once that's taken care of, I'll send out some guys and leave your pack to get settled in their accommodations as we wait for the Oaxaca pack's arrival. Once you are ready, you and your beta, Alpha Silver, as well as you Alpha Leo, can join me in my office to talk some things over."

They all nodded and after parting words and promises to meet up later, Leo steered me away.

"Where are we going," I asked as his arm slid from around my waist to grab my hand instead.

Leo nodded and said, "It is. Just try it. You'll like it, I promise."

So I did, and it was quite delicious. It was like granola and some other stuff. I think it was basically like muesli. I'd never tried it before, but I had heard of it and seen it in grocery stores.

I smiled at him gently to see him watching me with soft eyes, "Thank you."

He smiled back and said, "Of course, Mine. You keep seeming so surprised but I told you, you are and will always be my priority. No matter what it is."

I blushed. Not knowing how to respond I looked down and finished eating. After I was done I got down to go wash the bowl, spoon, and glass- ignoring his attempt at grabbing them from me.

It was refreshing to have someone take care of me but it didn't change the fact that I could still take care of myself.

As I finished, I looked over at him. "So, when are you needing to go meet Gabriel and Silver for that meeting?" At his frown, I shook my head and gently stopped him. "I know you don't like me saying their names. But please, it's weird enough saying their titles as it is. But I really don't want to say them more than I have to. Especially when I'm just talking to you."

He sighed begrudgingly and nodded, but dropped it. "In

about an hour. We will have another small one with the Oaxaca pack Alpha, as well. When he gets here, that is. But tomorrow we will have a larger one."

All of the alphas have been using this once in a lifetime chance to also try something they never really had a chance at before. They were drawing out plans and maps and writing out ways to stay in contact with each other better.

They had a very rudimentary base of knowledge of other packs before now. It was really just based on what they had known from the beginning of everything. Right after they became known to the world.

It was also helping them establish some other things they hoped to implement when the time was right. Such as a "pack meet" every 5 years to help keep communications up, and help to see if any mates were in other packs.

Though they are few and far between, there are daughters born in some of the packs right now. Though they will still be coming to Gabriel's territory to see if their mate is here, if they haven't found their mate, it wouldn't help to see if their mate is in another pack.

It was crazy they never tried to do something about that before. I mean, how many wolves had mates in other packs this entire time?

I shook my head to clear it.

But anyway, they hoped that every time a new alpha came they would be able to have these talks with them. In the hope they would all agree and can pass the information they gather to all the packs after. Unfortunately, that meant Leo was seemingly always in meetings.

His voice interrupted my thoughts, "So, what will you be doing when I am in this meeting? Are you going to try and talk to Ruby again?"

I shook my head, "No, I don't think I will. I already told her she can find me if she needed to talk but I don't think I'll go looking for her. Honestly, I don't really feel like that's the best thing for me to do. Besides, I'd rather not have a repeat of earlier."

Leo nodded and grew silent. I was a little concerned until he said, so softly I almost didn't hear him, "What you said earlier... about this world being horrible and unfair... I know it is. Or at least seems that way to you. But if you could get on a plane and somehow go back, would you?"

I stopped and stared at him. He had such a vulnerable look in his eyes and I knew he was scared.

I didn't want to upset him, but the truth was I didn't know the answer to his question. Then I thought about it.

If I had stayed there, or even gone back, I don't think I'd be able to live a happy life knowing what I know now. I wouldn't be able to have a mate. An honest-to-goodness soulmate. I may not even have had a family. I also would have had all of this knowledge that the world, essentially, was going to end as we knew it without any way to prove it or stop it.

No. Knowing what I know now, I don't think I could go back even if I could.

I looked up at him and saw the fear in his eyes as he stared at me. I smiled gently and leaned up to place a kiss on his cheek before looking into his eyes and responding, "I honestly don't know what is going to happen. Between the packs, between us, in this world. But it is my world now. Our world. Nothing is going to change that. But even if it could, no. No, I wouldn't go back."

The smile that lit his eyes before slowly spreading across his face was enough to make the day better. Even without tacos.

It let me know I had made the right choice.

What I had said was true. About not knowing what was going to happen. But I now began to actually see possibilities. Possibilities I didn't even see before I got on that plane.

Truly great possibilities.

CHAPTER THIRTEEN

One hour later I wandered into the library.

It was not really a library. At least, that was not what it looked like it had been. But, people now used it as a library and as a gathering room just to hang out.

Since I had time while Leo was in his meeting, I decided to explore some more. There really was not much else to do here.

The alphas still refused to let any of us 'Luna's go outside of the packhouse without an escort and I did not enjoy needing a babysitter.

I'm independent enough that I plan to revisit that subject with Leo when the time is right. But I knew there was no point in even trying to do that while there were still so many new packs arriving.

If there was one thing I was realizing the importance of, it was getting better at knowing when to pick my battles.

So, here I was, slowly looking at as many book titles as I could.

There was a surprising amount of genres spread out throughout the shelves. They were all older books- some of which I recognized by title and some I knew were old simply by looking at them. However, as old and used these books obviously were, they were still well taken care of.

It still was surprising to me just how much these people relied on things from basically a century ago to entertain themselves. I would think people would still be making new books.

I know it wasn't exactly a priority and I knew there wouldn't really be any mass distribution of books. But, like a few sets of books people can write in and keep info and records would be smart. So, I was surprised there were none.

The author in me perked up a little as a thought occurred to me.

Gabriel, Leo, and the other alphas were all collecting loads of data from each alpha. Like ways to communicate, their pack locations, and potential mates.

Maybe I could help write some books. Record keeping books for that information, but also maybe books with information about this world. Not just for those of us who are new to it but also those who are used to it. It seemed like a good idea and I was beginning to get excited about a project.

Then the smile which had begun to spread across my face stopped and I shook away the thought. I shouldn't get carried away. I could maybe ask to help Gabriel with keeping track of everything. Then I could also learn more about all of this world and the packs while I was doing it. But there were many more important things for me to focus on before I suddenly decided to settle down and start whiling away hours writing books.

I did not want any type of leadership position. I was just a person who happened to have had a hand in finding help for the rest of the plan survivors. Just a person who happened to somehow give a bunch of shifters a small glimmer of hope simply by being kidnapped and auctioned off to the man who was apparently made for me. But somehow I did become someone who was needed.

So, I would not simply get hung up on trying to settle down when there were so many things that needed to be done.

This *was* my world now. I mean, I got here somehow by crashing a plane. There were no planes for me to get on to try and crash back in time. Though I didn't particularly want to try and live through a second plane crash.

Also, I meant what I said to Leo earlier. But, it didn't mean I had to exactly sit back and get used to all of the bad things in this new world of mine.

Like the stupid 'Gathering' thing. I was not dumb enough to assume I would be able to do anything about it. Especially since it was not just something that happened here, but everywhere.

But I had to find a way to help those girls. Not just the girls that had been auctioned off with me, like the girl from the plane, but also the ones who would be captured in the future. Maybe even those who have already been captured.

I also had my most pressing concern, the survivors here.

Yes, we were all at a standstill with the promise to see if any survivors were the mates to any shifters. But that does not mean we have to all just stay here and twiddle our thumbs. Not now and definitely not in the future.

There had to be something I could do to fix this.

Just like how I was feeling bored and almost useless, I was sure the other survivors were feeling the same way. Just thinking about all this was beginning to stress me out. But I knew I had to do something.

I turned and with narrowed eyes, I decided I would first do the thing I could actually do. Which was to visit Gabriel.

He was probably still in his meeting with Leo, Silver, and the others. Which would make it an opportune time to find them and bring up my ideas.

Normally I didn't mind the fact they were all constantly having private meetings, simply because I would seriously be bored sitting in meetings listening to things I didn't even understand. But now I realized I wanted to learn. If I was to stay here I *needed* to learn.

But I also needed to find something for everyone to do. So we didn't grow stir crazy while we were here waiting for who knows how much longer.

I found my way out of the library and wandered through the house until I got to the door I knew was Gabriel's office door. I took a deep breath and knocked on it.

I had barely finished knocking when the door flew open so suddenly a squeak came out of me and I jumped a little.

Leo was on the other side and immediately was pulling me to him as his eyes wandered my body and demanded, "What is it? What's wrong?"

I relaxed and chuckled, shaking my head. I should have known he would hear or smell me, or however he always seemed to know where I was. But I also did not realize he would be so panicked, thinking something had to be wrong since I was here. In hindsight, I should have realized he would be concerned about my unusual appearance.

I reached over and gently placed a hand on his cheek, "Nothing is wrong. I actually came to join you guys."

I vaguely noticed the men in the room behind Leo wearing matching expressions of shock. Silver looked amused though, as well as Leo.

"Join us? That's...okay. I won't say that's unusual because, well, I wouldn't know. But it is surprising. You never seemed interested in joining before."

Leo slightly turned and looked at Gabriel with an eyebrow raised, "If that's okay?"

Gabriel was watching Leo and me with a blank expression.

I shifted on my feet a little, unsure of this reception. I had not thought me coming to talk would be an issue and I would respect his opinion if he wanted me to leave. I wouldn't like it, but I would respect it.

I released a small breath of air I had not realized I had been holding when Gabriel finally nodded and said, "Come in, Luna Ava." He waited until I came in and Leo shut the door once more to ask, "May I ask why you would like to join us? I know Ana doesn't really like to partake in alpha affairs herself. I had just assumed it would be the same for someone who did not really know what we would be discussing."

I smiled sheepishly as I held Leo's hand. Not that I had a choice because I could tell he did not like the idea of letting me go now that I was in a room full of other men. "I actually didn't really want to join your meetings before for that very reason. But I realized I have a lot of questions and if this is to be my new world then I need to learn. But that's only really an added benefit to why I wanted to come. I actually had a proposition."

I saw some of the men settle against their seats or the wall where they were standing and swallowed a little.

I was kind of nervous and did not feel excited about the prospect of them laughing at what I had to say, but as I looked around I realized they all were staring in encouragement. Or at least not in discouraging ways.

"So, in the time I came from I was an author. I wrote books. Not really anything important but there are some benefits to the job. I had to be good at writing, obviously, but there's so much more to that. Researching and collecting data, analyzing facts, recognizing patterns, planning... there's so much more to it. But when I was in your library earlier an idea came to mind. Multiple ideas really but... still. I know you guys are trying to build a record system of sorts with all the alphas."

I paused, staring at them and biting my lip, "Anyway, I figured I could help you. Write a book of sorts. I noticed you guys don't really have any record-keeping going on. At least, not in the library. It will help keep all of the information organized and in one place. And once you get new or more information you can just add to it. But I can help get you started. I can even help ask some other plane people if they want to. Or even help set up something like a working system for them."

Gabriel shifted and glanced at Leo, "Well, that would be very helpful of you. To sit in and write for us. We have been trying to keep up with a lot of our information tracking, but I am kinda ashamed to mention that a book never came to mind. But, I don't know about inviting others to help. If you really need help we can try, maybe Ana. But I don't know how I feel about humans knowing our secrets."

"Well, we are humans too. And they really need something to be doing soon, I'm sure. I'm going stir crazy here and I'm actually in a house where I can learn to cook or watch movies or read books. Most of the others are stuck outside in tents. I mean, some of them have found jobs for themselves with washing clothes and helping heal. But I'm sure they have to be getting bored soon if they aren't already."

I felt Leo shift next to me and I heard him say, "I think she has a point. Though I agree with you on who can help keep books and be in on our meetings," he glanced at me, "Yes you are humans, but you are also our mates and Luna's. Our secrets are now your secrets. As much as I would love to hope most of the others end up being mates and even accepting their mates if they are, it probably won't be that many of them. There's only so much we can share with humans. That's how we stay safe. Stay alive."

My eyes widened in understanding and I slowly nodded. *Okay.* That made sense and I should have realized that before.

Leo looked back over at Gabriel, "But I do see what she's trying to say. It'll probably also help them settle and be a bit more okay with staying in one place for as long as we need them to if they have something to keep them busy."

I nodded and as an idea came to me I joined in, "It doesn't have to be anything too busy or important. I mean, I know many of them are still healing. But they could help cook, or learn to cook or repair clothes if they can. We can help actually designate people to help clean around here or wash clothes. Heck, even training people how to survive. I know you guys may not be that crazy about trying to train us weak human beings to fight or find ingredients but we will all need to know that. Whether we are Shifter mates or not."

I shook my head, "Anyway, there *are* things we can do. Both to be helpful around here and things to learn. It just needs to be planned and organized. But also to help all of us not feel so cooped up. It shouldn't be hard to figure that out. We can ask around about what people would be interested in learning and what they already can do."

Leo squeezed my hand and I looked up at him to find him smiling at me.

I blushed and dipped my head a little but couldn't stop myself from smiling at the look of pride in his eyes. I could practically hear him saying something about me being and acting like a Luna. But I was just doing what was right; what should be done.

Silver's voice caught my attention and I looked up in enough time to catch his wink my way, "I can help teach a cooking class or two while I'm here. I know a certain beautiful lady who would sign up already!"

Leo's growl broke the room's relative silence, as well as the chuckles from the others which followed.

I winked back and grinned cheekily, "Sign me up!"

Leo practically yanked me to his side and growled out, "Not without me."

I laughed and glanced up at him, "I would also enjoy learning how to fight. If we can work something out like that."

I could tell Leo did not appreciate the idea and was probably about to say so, but I squeezed his hand and said softly, "Please, Leo. I need to know. And as much as you would love to always protect me from everything, there will be times you may not. Besides, we can have some pack members train everyone else while you train me yourself!"

Leo's eyes narrowed as he looked at me but I knew he wasn't going to finish talking about this in front of the others. I was just happy to take the slight win I got simply by him not saying no.

He looked at the others and then asked Gabriel, "So, what do you think about all this?"

Gabriel leaned back in the chair behind his desk. It was a big desk and all the furniture looked like many offices I was used to seeing.

A big desk sat in the middle of the room, a chair behind it and a few chairs in front of it, a long couch against the wall, and a bookshelf that was around nine feet tall on the wall behind the desk. But in two corners there were things like sconces on the walls, with fire lighting the room with the help of a lantern on the corner of his desk.

There was also something I thought was cool. The whole wall behind the desk, that the bookshelf was in the middle of, was painted with chalk paint I had seen before- along with the wall opposite of the one the couch was on and the wall the door was on. There was some chalk writing scrambled all over it and I realized it was how Gabriel had been keeping track of things, specifically his pack schedules and now all of the information he was getting from other pack alphas.

It was a cool way to keep track of things that were always changing. But probably not the safest way to keep track of things of importance and things he wanted to keep secret. Seeing as things could be erased and this was the office he was using to have meetings in.

I was pulled from my thoughts to see Gabriel watching me. His lips twitched in what looked like almost a smile, and he said, "I can see the benefit of training you guys on what we can, and finding some things to keep you busy while you are still here. I won't step in your way with whatever else you are wanting to do. But I *would* appreciate your help in at least starting us a book to help keep up with all this info we are gathering if you can. As long as you run things by me that are of high importance and only receive help from those who can know about it. None of the information can be passed along to an outsider."

I nodded with a small smile, "Okay. Well, I'll need some writing material and things. I'll actually need some time to think about what I'll need to get started. Maybe the rest of the day. But while I'm at it, I'll also try to figure out how to get something started with everyone outside."

Gabriel nodded and the room fell silent again.

I rocked back on my heels a little and bit my lip. "Well, okay then, I guess I'll leave you guys to finish the rest of your meeting while I get started."

Gabriel gave me a soft smile and nod, and Silver gave me a quick thumbs up. I looked up at Leo to say goodbye but stopped when he opened the door and pulled me out with him.

I looked at him in shock when he threw over his shoulder, "I'm going to help her. I'll see you later when the Oaxaca pack arrives."

Without waiting for a response, he pulled me away and smiled down at me with a shake of his head. He had a look in his eyes that looked like awe and amusement, and he just whispered, "My Luna."

I blushed and shook my head, and then set off on my new mission. Finding writing material in the year 2144. Sounded like a piece of cake.

Not.

CHAPTER FOURTEEN

Finding lots of unused and non-ruined paper was proving to be slightly difficult. Finding scraps of paper in different places to at least get started on making lists was another story.

After finding a piece of paper in semi-decent shape with no writing on the back, I wrote out a notice so I wouldn't have to keep repeating myself or try to remember the people's responses.

"Notice:

We are looking for interests and talents! This way we can use what we know to help out around here, and learn what we don't know!

Please write your name and any skill sets you have on the left column (like sewing, making candles, making soap, cooking, etc.). And please write your name and what you may be interested in doing/learning in the right column (like hunting, gardening, cooking, self-defense, etc.)...

Columns are on the paper below!"

Once I was done, I used a couple of tacks I found in Gabriel's office to push the papers onto the tree that many people tend to pass between the house and the tents that had been set up.

Hopefully, it was in a well-noticed location. Even if it wasn't, I was about to go let everyone know about it.

I figured this was probably the smartest approach. Instead of asking what people were willing to do first, I could first figure out what people could do or were interested in doing.

There was plenty of semi-used paper, chalk, and even some markers in Gabriel's office. He even had some organization supplies that would help- like tacks, strings, and ways to color-code things. Just about everything I needed could be found here, along with using the chalk walls to help gather my thoughts and organize them before actually putting them on paper. But I still did need books to write in.

If I had to, I could create those make-shift books I vaguely remembered having to do in elementary school. Though they were roughly designed and not the best option for long-term use. Nevertheless, I had hoped that there may be journals or something that are still able to be found in some nearby towns.

Another thing to add to the list for when some of the pack members go to town later.

The list keeps growing longer and longer, and the shifters would surely not be enjoying their trip with how many things they will be needing to try and find. But it couldn't be helped.

Silver had briefly mentioned to me in passing, after the meeting earlier, that he was not sure if he would be able to give me the cooking lessons I wanted until he saw just how many ingredients they could find.

It was more a question of what they could find to determine what we would have time to make, than the ingredients themselves.

Silver was so 'normal' that I enjoyed talking to him and looked forward to getting to know him. But it probably *would* have to wait until those lessons because anytime we talked Leo got all growly and possessive. Sometimes it was cute. Sometimes it was so annoying I wanted to slap his arm and ignore him. But, after my brief talks with Ana, I knew Leo was just doing what was natural for shifters.

Though, I did look forward to hanging out with Silver some more. He reminded me of Marcus in personality but seemed even more normal compared to everyone else.

I had asked him earlier how he spoke English so well. Not just in words but also understanding English well. He had briefly mentioned that his pack had mainly settled in the Sonora area of Mexico, but their pack territory technically reached as far as areas in California and Arizona. So just about everyone in their pack grew up speaking both Spanish and English.

When I got the chance I planned on asking him more about it because it seemed very interesting to me.

I may even have to start collecting written recipes down if the practical aspect of our cooking lessons ended up not available for us to do here. That could be our make-shift cooking lessons with the practical aspect being me simply learning through trial and error on my own. With so many packs coming from so many places I really could learn a lot. Maybe even write a cookbook!

I shook my head and chuckled to myself. My mind always goes straight to books.

I turned around and walked toward the tents where Leo was waiting already. Leo was very rarely away from me. He only ever left my side when he had a meeting with Gabriel and, if I had to wager on it, I would bet he would not even leave me for those if I told him I wanted him to stay. At least, not simply stating I wanted him to stay but actually asking him to. I honestly could not imagine why I would though. I didn't need to have him by my side all day every day. Besides, I would probably be sitting in on the meetings now. For the most part. So, even those moments of separation will soon be decreasing in time.

I shook my head again as I reached him.

He must have been able to read the look on my face because

he chuckled as he reached for my hand. "Hello, Mine. Can't get rid of me that easily. Ready to go in?"

I rolled my eyes in amusement at his statement but held his hand back and nodded. "Ready as I'll ever be."

When we ducked into the biggest tent that was being used mainly for the plane survivors, I took a second to look around. My life has changed so much recently.

Was it really just two weeks ago I was shut in my room, being completely antisocial with no one really to call 'my people'? I was perfectly fine with that life. Well, not necessarily perfectly fine. I would have loved to have had things like a boyfriend or friends who really understood me. But here I was, two weeks later, and my life was completely different. It could not get any more different.

But, ignoring the obvious changes, I now had everything I had wanted and more in a way. I had two groups of people I belonged to and a man in my life.

If only, other than Leo, I wanted it. I chuckled to myself. I was one of those cliche people who finally got what I wanted and wanted to escape from it constantly.

Sighing, I realized I should probably grab their attention. Though we already were in some way, seeing as many people seemed to have stopped what they were doing to stare at us.

I took a shaky breath and my hand tightened around Leo's. I did not even realize it until his hand squeezed mine and then his thumb began to stroke my hand in reassurance.

Leo's voice was loud as it rang out through the tent. Not because he yelled but because his voice carried and seemed to have a presence of its own. It was probably something he got from being an alpha. But his voice itself seemed to capture everyone's attention even as he asked for it.

"Hello everyone. I know we have not been around as I am sure you would appreciate. I just take responsibility for keeping Ava away. Just as you are all settling in here, she is settling in alongside me and I must admit I am quite protective of my time with her," he smiled sheepishly. "Still, we didn't exactly come to hang out. If you will, please give my mate your attention. Thank you."

He looked down at me and I stared at the room with burning cheeks and wide eyes. The squeeze of his hand on mine once more knocked me out of the mini freak out I was currently having.

I cleared my throat but my voice still came out slightly hoarse, "Um yeah. Sorry guys. I uh... well I had an idea today and have run it by Alpha Gabriel and well... I don't know about you guys, but I am super stir crazy here. Who knows how much longer we will all be here but I figured you guys probably felt the same. So, I figured we can simultaneously start helping out around here, as well as maybe learning some new things to settle into our new lives here."

Licking my lips I cleared my throat again, "I found some paper and posted a make-shift signup sheet on that-uh- the central tree outside. You know, the one you pass going up to the main house? Anyway, if you guys have any special skills and can help out, you can let us know. Or if you have anything that you probably *need* to learn now in this... new world of ours, then you can also request that there. Like learning how to fight or find ingredients out in the wild. You know, stuff like that. It's not a guarantee or anything but -uh- yea... it's a start and it'll help give us something to do while we are here."

I looked up at him again, smiling gratefully as his words caused everyone to stop staring.

I sucked in a deep breath as I finished. I *hated* speaking to groups of people. Especially as the center of attention.

No one said anything as they stared at me and I slowly began to panic. Leo chuckled, "Well, that's all we came here to let you guys know. Not much to it."

Some people returned to what they were doing and others got up to head past us out of the tent with some smiles or whispers of "great idea" aimed my way.

I was smiling when movement in the corner of the tent caught my eye.

Ruby.

She stood there with a look on her face I could not really figure out. Then she slowly leaned away from the wall, gave me a small smile, and left.

I was not sure what that meant but I was assuming she was not ready to talk yet.

I felt like a horrible person because I was relieved she had not come towards us to talk. I *would* talk to her when she was ready. But even though it felt like it was days ago already, it was hard to forget her outburst had only happened that morning.

I did not enjoy the idea of revisiting that topic on the same day it had happened, if she happened to still be thinking the same thoughts.

I did not think she meant it. But sometimes it was hard to remember she was still a girl who was suddenly ripped away from her family and friends. I mean, she *was* 18 years old and we were all ripped away from everything we knew. But she and the two kids who had survived the plane crash must be having a particularly difficult time.

Then again, most kids tend to be resilient when given the opportunity.

So, I was sure she would feel better once she calmed down and realized there was no going back, that she had to learn to adjust to her new life. Once she realized this was probably one of the safest places for us to be right now I *would* be there to help her through that when she needed me. Even if I had to take her back with me to Leo's pack after.

If she wanted to, of course, and did not end up having a mate.

Thinking of the other two kids made me want to check on them and see how they were doing. If I remember correctly, one of them had been traveling by themself on the plane and the other had been traveling with both of her parents. One parent had passed away in the crash itself and the other was one of the people who happened to have passed away when I had left looking for help.

Both of the kids seemed to have taken to staying together and we had tried to get them to stay up at the main house in one of the rooms when we first got here. But the girl who had lost both of her parents had not spoken a word since then and we did not want to try and separate the two of them.

The boy, who had been traveling by himself, was 10 years old and named Liam. I had never understood why parents would let their little kid travel on a plane without them, but his parents probably would regret their decision for the rest of their lives.

The girl, however, was a teenager. Since we could not get her to speak we didn't know how old she was yet or her name. But we were pretty sure she wasn't of mating age- meaning old enough for her mate to be able to tell she was his mate. At least, she looked younger than 16 to me and she had yet to find her mate. But she was not exactly meeting all the wolves who were coming through either.

I just wish I could get her to say something. I had tried to talk to her a little when I could, but I had not been down to the tent in a while and she did not come up to the house. She kind of just stayed in her makeshift bed most of the time.

I whispered to Leo that I would be right back and walked to the back of the main tent, passing by the makeshift door to the sleeping quarters, and headed to where her bed was.

I could see Liam chatting away softly to her, telling her all of the things that were going on around the territory. I could tell she was listening to him simply by the intelligent and analytical gleam in her eyes, but she didn't respond.

Liam's voice broke off when I approached and then a big grin spread across his face as he chirped hello to me.

Smiling, I sat down on the edge of the cot across from them and said softly, "Hi Liam. Do you remember me? I haven't had the chance to visit in a while."

He answered in a voice that made me think he really wanted to say duh. "Of course. You're the one they all talk about who saved us."

I chuckled, " I am. Though, I'm not really the person who saved you guys. But that is what they call me." I glanced over at the girl slowly and softly asked, "How are you guys today?"

I didn't react outwardly but I was shocked when her eyes slowly moved to meet mine.

That hasn't happened before.

I paused, almost feeling like a hunter who does not want to scare the animal they were hunting. Whatever she was or was not about to do, I did not want to say or do something and ended up stopping her.

There was a very small, almost imperceptible, tilt of her lips before she looked down.

Not realizing I had tensed up, I slowly relaxed once I realized that was all I was going to get from her. It was not much, but it was more than I had gotten before.

Gently clearing my throat I slowly stood up. "Well, I will let you guys get back to whatever you were doing before. But our offer still stands. If you guys wanna come up to sleep in an actual room- in an actual bed- at the main house, you can. Just let me know and I'll make it happen. It might be nice for you guys. Have a nice bath or shower, and a comfy place to sleep."

After a few moments of a long drawn-out, and admittedly awkward, silence I nodded and said bye to them, then left.

Leaving that section of the tent, I met up with Leo who was talking to the doctor of our group. When I had somehow gotten the position of being a delegate between the survivors and pack, I had noticed the doctor seemed to be the real leader of our motley group of strangers. Something I was more than fine with.

The older man smiled gently at me as I approached. "That was a good idea, Ava. Though many are still healing and will be for a while, or helping do small things around here, I have noticed people getting restless. It'll also help if we can find some way for those who are feeling better but still confined to their bed to be productive. So they aren't trying to move before they need to."

I blushed a little in embarrassment but waved a hand in the air, "Oh it was nothing. Honestly, I only thought about it because I was bored."

The doctor chuckled. "That's alright. At times, I myself am bored. Not necessarily because I have nothing to do, but more because none of us are really used to only doing one thing and one thing only. But still, it was a nice idea. One that has me thinking, maybe I could even help train some of the Shifters in some of the medical aspects."

He looked over at Leo with a slightly sheepish look on his face. "Not that I am saying you all don't know how to do things. I'm sure you guys have some kind of knowledge to have survived this long, but I'm sure I know some things you guys don't."

Leo smiled at the doctor. "No, you are right. We do know some things that managed to be passed down or that we learned through trial and error. But I'm sure many people would enjoy learning more from you. I will let Alpha Gabriel know your suggestion. Maybe other packs would even be interested and you can have people to train from other packs, as well."

I perked up a little, "Great idea! Like a mentoring program!"

The doctor chuckled, "Yes, a mentoring program. That would probably help keep me busy once I don't have patients like I do now."

Someone called for him from somewhere near the tarp-like door separating the main area from where I knew the beds were for those still healing.

I nodded and said goodbye as the doctor looked at us and said, "Excuse me. Duty calls."

As Leo and I walked out of the tent I told him about my little side trip to see the kids.

"I'm concerned for the girl. But I think she is slowly starting to get better. I was thinking, if they are up for it, maybe we can get her to participate in something. Like maybe when Silver and I are cooking. If we can. I don't know."

He pulled me to him and placed a gentle kiss on my head, "I think that's a great idea if she is interested. I think she just needs some time to come to terms with everything. I'm thinking along the same lines with Ruby. You can't push them to suddenly be okay and adapt to everything. Heck, you and some of the others have done better than I would have thought you would. But they will get better. It's just something they need to do themselves."

I nodded in agreement. It was something I had thought of to myself, so I knew he was right. It did not make things easier though.

I shook my head to clear my thoughts, "Do you know when the Shifters Gabriel is sending to see if they can find the ingredients and supplies we need are getting back?"

It was close an hour or so before the sun was going to set. At least, that's what it looked like to me. So, the Oaxaca pack could not be *that* far away from arriving. So, it would kind of help if they got back soon so we could know if we would be having the taco night or not. But, also, I did my best writing at night.

It would be cool if I could get started that night on some of my many book ideas I had.

Leo shook his head, "Not really. Unfortunately, it's hard to put an actual time on their trip because none of us know whether they will find things or not. Or how many places they will be looking through. But, I'm sure Alpha Gabriel and Luna Ana have ideas in mind for dinner. I must admit, it feels quite nice for me to not have to worry about things like that while we are here." He chuckled and gave me a wry grin. "Right now, Marcus is dealing with all of that for our pack. I'm sure he's going to whine for days once we get back."

My eyes widened slightly, "Oh poor Marcus! Who knows how long we will be here."

Leo laughing with a little evil-looking grin on his face made me roll my eyes. But I couldn't help but laugh along with him. For an alpha wolf, he sure did act like a little boy sometimes.

Shaking my head I said, "Okay, let's get inside. You can help me start writing all of that stuff on the walls in Gabriel's office down on some paper. That way, if they happen to find some empty books or journals, I can start writing it all down from our room tonight."

Leo took my hand and nodded, "Okay. Anything for you, Mine." He grinned and winked at me.

I rolled my eyes in amusement but shook my head. I swear life would never be boring with him by my side. If for no other reason than his crazy attempts at getting 'brownie points'.

CHAPTER FIFTEEN

Time seemed to go by fast after that.

It has been almost a week without Ruby saying more than a passing word. She hasn't blown up again and smiles at me when we pass each other, but I know she's not happy.

I really do not understand what caused her to get so upset. At least, to the point that it has been a week and there has been no difference.

Other than Ruby, though, there have been a lot of changes this past week.

After posting the sign about people's skills and what they desire to learn, many people had gotten involved in makeshift groups all around the territory. Many wolves coming through even have been taking some time to add their knowledge during one group's session or another's. It has definitely seemed to help people get moving and become a little more settled.

I also managed to get the two kids from the plane crash to finally move up into a room in the main house. They are still sleeping in the same room as each other, but it is progressing. Even if the girl is still just 'the girl' because she still has not talked.

I have also had many tacos over the span of one week. Granted it is not quite like what I think of when I think of tacos, it's still amazing to have it. Though I *would* love to have some sour cream.

The Oaxaca pack had come and gone, along with several other packs from around the world. The Sonoma pack left as well, though Silver was still here.

I enjoyed hanging out with him and learning all kinds of things, despite Leo's annoyance. He said he needed to make a trip to check out his pack's territory in the Old Arizona and California territories anyway. Yet, he had not left Gabriel's pack grounds so far.

I did not mind, though. Silver was keeping busy- helping Ana and me with the garden, teaching everyone about the safety of food in the wilderness and how to make ingredients for foods he taught us. He even helped Leo with my self-defense training. At least verbally since Leo was not letting any other guy get close enough to touch me.

But the reason why I did not mind having Silver around longer was because of the lending ear he gave me with Ruby still not really talking to me. Do not get me wrong, Leo is always more than willing to listen but it's nice to have someone else to talk to also. Ana is nice to talk to but it's just a convenience type thing at this point. But Silver understands more than the others do. Maybe it is because his pack is used to cultural differences anyway. Maybe it is because being an Alpha of such a big and constantly moving pack could be difficult without having someone to talk to yourself. I don't know. But I do know, he will make some lady really lucky one day.

Over the past week, I have also been helping out with the record-keeping of meetings with all of the Alphas.

I internally laugh every time I think of it. If you had told me six months ago I would be going from a bestselling author to a glorified minute-taker for werewolves... well I would have probably turned it into a book.

However, it was not only important but was also helping me to learn about wolf shifter packs better than I could otherwise.

I also was getting closer to Leo and the idea of finally becoming his mate in more than just name. Or, at least, running out of excuses about pushing it off. Not that Leo would say anything about it. But I do know he is getting more restless about the fact he has not claimed me yet. Especially with the number of men constantly coming.

One day, one of the few times I was having a cooking lesson with Silver that Leo was not at, I had talked to Silver about mates. I figured it would be nice to learn about it from a guy's point of view who was not going to pull his punches, so to speak.

When we think about what we have read in books about werewolves or shapeshifters with their mates, it is all true for the most part. Their one true love is bound to lead to possessive and protective tendencies emerging in a species filled with animalistic characteristics. But adding that on top of very few people even finding their mates now and I can see how that would make it worse to not have your mark on your mate for others to see. It helped me to see how Leo may be really feeling about how we are waiting.

"Hey, what are you thinking about?"

I jumped and swung around to see Leo standing there watching me. I guess I had been so caught up in my thoughts I didn't hear him come in.

"Oh! Hey. I-uh, nothing really. Just how fast this week's gone by. Why?" It looked like he had an actual reason to ask and was not just wondering. Which was just as well seeing how I probably would not want to tell him, "*Oh, nothing. Just the fact I am still wrapping my head around everything, including being your mate, and even though I think I may be starting to fall for you and I know how much it is upsetting you to wait to mate with me, I still don't know if I'm ready.*"

Yeah, I'm a rambler and a serious run-on type of thinker.

Even if it is just in my head. But really. How does one even know when they're ready to irrevocably tie down their life to another? Especially when they have not even known that person long.

Yep. So not saying that to him.

When I blinked out of my thoughts once more I noticed Leo watching me with a slightly tilted head and a small curve to his lips. "I know there's more to it but I'll let you keep your secrets, Mine."

He walked over and sat next to me. "I wanted to let you know one of Gabriel's pack members is going back into their nearby town. If you need anything, he is leaving within the next hour."

I frowned a little. "Why is he going back into town so soon?"

Leo blinked and looked away evasively, "Just needing to look for something."

I narrowed my eyes. "Leo. Tell me. Please. We promised to be open and honest. That's the only way this will ever work between us." It was a low blow. Despite honesty being an important aspect of our relationship, if he really did not want to tell me why someone was going to the town that was his prerogative. I would not necessarily be happy about it and would try to find out, but I would not be mad enough to let it fester.

He grumbled and stretched his head then ran his hand through his hair while he shifted. "Okay, fine. I didn't want to worry you but there apparently have been some rumblings amongst the town humans. Somehow they learned about there being a group of humans here. But they were told the humans were being held against their will."

I raised my eyebrow.

"Okay. Yea, they kind of are. But that's because we agreed upon it. So they kind of aren't."

I chuckled a little, "I know. I know. I was just messing with you." But then the smile fell from my lips. "I really don't know how they'd know about any of this anyway. Or why they'd care."

"Well, about why they'd care. Well, that's not something

super shocking. Sadly, it's more to do with potential women that we are getting first chances with than humans being here. This world we live in is not always bad but it is not always good."

"The 'how they know' part of that sentence is what we would like to know also. The only way would be for someone from here to tell them or one of the town humans come here. Neither option makes sense. We haven't let anyone other than pack members leave recently and the pack guards would have been able to scent any human who doesn't belong after this much time getting acclimated to your time's humans."

I shake my head, "So, someone told them things that aren't true. Or at least exaggerated versions of the truth. But I don't understand who would do that. Why? And it sounds like if you're sure no stranger can get here undetected the only option is someone got out without anyone knowing. But I don't understand why any of the plane survivors would do that. Not only did you guys save them, but this past week has seemed great!"

Sighing in frustration Leo answered. "I agree. That's what is so frustrating and why Gabriel is sending someone. He's hoping we can either find out how they found out or find a way to defuse the situation. The last thing we need is this leading to a situation where they try to come here to take people."

"I just don't see how anyone would do this," I groan and massage my temple. "I really don't."

Standing up, Leo holds out a hand. "Come on. Let's go meet up with the others downstairs. They're probably all talking about it in Alpha Gabriel's office right now."

I chuckle and roll my eyes at him still using Gabriel's title but take his hand to follow. "Okay. I just hope there's something we've overlooked and it's not someone here trying to cause problems."

Kissing my forehead and pulling me out the door of our bedroom, Leo agrees with me.

When we got downstairs it was to a lot of raised voices that even I, a human, could hear through the thick wooden door of

Gabriel's office. Not so much as yelling at each other as it was people with differing opinions trying to be heard over others.

Walking in, I was shocked to see a few humans in the office as well as quite a few shifters. Two of whom were the Doctor and Ruby. The latter was even more shocking to me, seeing how she had made it no secret how she felt about being here.

A strange feeling went through my body but I shook it off. I was just being paranoid.

Seeing us enter the room, silence fell. Until Gabriel broke it from his place behind his chair, standing with his hands on Ana's shoulders. "So, we are sending a runner into town to try and find a way to fix things from that end while we increase our border patrol units. As you can see, Alpha Leo, Luna Ava, we decided this situation was important enough to let the humans here know. If we are unable to de-escalate this situation or find who caused it in the first place, it is highly problematic. When I say this, I mean it. Not just for us but also for all of you humans from the past. These humans here, the ones getting all angry over you being kept in our territory, are not getting angry because of any humane reason. They're angry because there are females here and they want females. It is as simple as that. They will try and kill the human males just as much as they'll try and kill us shifters. They'll steal the women and, at best, sell them to The Gathering. At worst, they'll rape and pass the females along to each other. This is a serious and potentially deadly problem for all of us here."

There were lots of murmurs after that statement, mainly from the humans in the room.

"Quiet. Please." Gabriel's voice interrupted them in a barely raised voice, but once which carried. "I am not saying this to scare you. Though being aware enough of the situation to be scared is necessary."

With a furrowed brow I spoke. "In all honesty, I feel the only way we may be able to de-escalate this situation is to somehow make them stand down. I'm sure many of the town people don't want to cause problems with your pack. You said before you guys were particularly close to each other since you protect them. So, why would they even be ruining all of that simply based on a rumor?"

Ana shifted and spoke, "I was thinking that as well. We've never had a problem with them before."

I saw many of the shifters nod and murmur in agreement.

"I believe it's not the humans of the town that are making the situation into... well, a situation. Apparently, some men came through a couple of weeks ago. They are Gatherers. What we call the people who kidnap women for The Gathering. Now, we nor the town never let them do business or take women from around here. But we can't exactly run them off for doing nothing. I think these men are the ones who heard this rumor and are trying to rile up enough people to do something."

At Gabriel's words, the noise level in the office was once more filled with loud voices and growls.

"Wait. Wait! So, that's good don't you see? If they are in fact the people adding fuel to the fire, and the town's people already don't like them, then just use that to diffuse the situation!" I raised my voice to speak over the noise.

Leo nodded, his arm wrapping around my waist. "My mate is right. Most of us stay clear of the humans around our pack territories but you have told us you have a much friendlier arrangement with the town. A mutually beneficial one. The town won't want to risk that simply based on the words of untrustworthy outsiders if you can find a way to prove to them it's a lie."

Gabriel nodded. "That's a good idea. But how do we prove to them it's a lie? We don't let them come to our territory. For safety reasons, as I'm sure you understand. The same reason is why we've been keeping the plane survivors here and not letting them go into town a lot. So how do we convince them it's false, knowing that? And how do we do that before any action is taken?"

Just then Gabriel's Beta walked in. I had not realized he was missing until now but, by the look on his face, I could tell there was a good reason for his absence. Or a very bad one.

Ignoring everyone, he looked towards Gabriel. "I'm sorry, Alpha. But I have some news. I was speaking with the pack members we sent for the supply run last week and they remembered something they heard in town about a rash of women being kidnapped randomly throughout the entire country."

"What do you mean women being kidnapped randomly? Gatherers? Why are we just now hearing of this?" Gabriel demanded in a snarl.

His Beta and many other pack members lowered their heads a little in what I could only assume was a submissive gesture.

"They didn't recall it until now and at the time thought it was either just a tale being spread around or a positive thing. See, it's not Gatherer's. In fact, apparently, all of these women who are being kidnapped are victims of The Gathering themselves. The people they're being taken from are their buyers."

Shocked silence filled the room but I was intrigued. "That's a good thing, then! Isn't it? These women are being rescued!"

The Beta shook his head. "No, Luna Ava. It is. But not for us. Right now this story is just hearsay. Enough evidence to know women are being kidnapped but nothing else. Despite the humans in the nearby town not condoning the kidnapping of women and The Gathering, they won't stand by and allow any type of kidnapping. Even if it's from those who are victims of The Gathering trying to escape. At least, not publicly."

"But I don't understand. That's crazy! It shouldn't matter if these women want to escape by any means they can. If they really are being rescued then I'm assuming only the women who need to leave are being rescued. The ones who are in terrible situations!"

Gabriel growled. "While I agree. What does this have to do with our immediate situation?"

His Beta cleared his throat. "Right. Well, see, whoever spread the word or however they learned of the humans staying here, they weren't exactly told where these humans came from. So, they heard the rumor of the women who have been going missing for the past 6 months now and then heard of the sudden appearance of a group of humans being held here. Now, the townspeople may actually be giving some credibility to these rumors. What I'm saying is, it may not even be about the fact we have a group of humans as much as it is they think we are kidnapping women and holding them here."

Ana and Ruby gasped while all of the men growled or yelled. My eyes widened and I looked up at Leo. "This situation just got much more serious. We need to figure something out now."

Leo opened his mouth to say something as a muffled scream from outside filled the air and the scent of smoke wafted from under the office door.

"I think it's too late for that."

CHAPTER SIXTEEN

At once, chaos ensued. Many of the room's occupants ran out, heading towards the front door. Gabriel was pulling Ana towards a different direction than everyone else but I did not have a chance to see where. Leo was holding me to him trying to tell me something while I was trying to go see what was happening.

"Ava!," he practically roared. My attention snapped back to him and I stared with wide eyes. Not because of him yelling my name but because my mind was racing so fast I could not latch on to any singular thought. At least, I couldn't until his yell snapped me out of it.

"Stop and listen to me! I know you want to go out there right now. But I can't figure out what's happening and help if I'm worried about you."

I opened my mouth to protest. We did not even know what was happening outside yet. Not definitively. People could be hurt and they needed help!

But he cut me off before I got the chance to say any of that.

"Please Ava, Mine. I need you and Ruby to go grab the children from upstairs and then meet Ana down in the basement. There's a safe room down there that the pack has set up. She'll help you get there. Please. Do it for me." His voice was pleading but slightly distant. I could tell he was half paying attention to what was going on outside. But I still felt like I could help. Many of the people from the plane wreck were out there still. They needed to get to safety also. Frustration was building in me at him not understanding that I could not simply get myself to safety when others needed help.

"If you won't stay inside and be safe for me, do it for the children. They need help and what if something has happened. Ruby can't do it on her own." Just like that, the frustration at the entire situation deflated inside me. At least, in the way that had been building up to me insisting on going with him.

He was right. Ana was, I'm sure, gathering everyone she could. But who was getting the kids? I highly doubt Ana would even be thinking about them. Simply because she was not used to thinking about them, if not for the assumption someone else would get them. They needed to be the top priority.

I internally groaned in irritation. Then I sighed aloud, accepting he was right. At least to the point of making sure the children were safe. "Fine. But be safe! And the second you know it's safe come and get me! Or I'll come myself. People may need help!"

He nodded but I could tell he was growing increasingly distracted and relieved I agreed without much reluctance. He kissed me hard on the lips quickly then nodded toward Ruby.

She was standing in the corner of the room looking frightened. I hadn't even realized she was still here until he mentioned and motioned to her.

"Now go. Both of you. Get the kids and go to the basement. Ana will know what to do. Be safe, Mine. Or I'll make you eat dinner with everyone the rest of the time we're here."

I rolled my eyes but inwardly chuckled. I knew he would not make me do it if I did not want to. But I was growing increasingly aware that Leo was the kind of man who would not do anything to hurt me, even if he was joking. So, that was his way of simultaneously trying to let me know he was serious while making me feel better.

I grabbed Ruby by the hand and practically dragged her towards the stairs. We really did need to hurry. I had no clue what was going on outside but the smell of smoke was getting stronger. The sounds of yelling weren't as loud, but I wasn't sure if that was a good thing. "Come on! We need to get Liam and the girl! Hurry!"

When this was all over with, I was going to make it my mission to get the girl's name. I was tired of calling her 'the girl'. Both in my head and aloud.

Finally seeming to shake out of whatever funk she was in, Ruby nodded and ran up the stairs behind me. Through the window, I can see someone had lit a few trees on fire. *Gosh, that is so dangerous. How are we going to put the fire out? And before it spreads,* I thought to myself. It wasn't like we had fire stations. Or did we? There was still so much to this world I needed to learn.

Shaking my head, I cleared my thoughts. Now was not the time to panic or think about any of that.

Reaching the room we had given the kids to stay in, I opened the door to see no one. "Liam! Where are you guys?! Liam!" Looking over at Ruby I tried to contain my growing panic, "They're not here, and not answering!"

Ruby's eyes widened in concern. I could tell she was realizing what I did. They did not wander off without anyone. Ever. The girl barely even came out of the room and Liam did not like to leave her. I watched her back up a step and look both ways down the hallway. "You check here more! Look in all the possible hiding spots! I'll start looking in other rooms. Maybe they're just scared and hiding!"

I nodded, impressed with how she figured out they may be hiding somewhere when she had just seemed like she was in shock moments ago. "Okay! I'll look in other rooms after this one. You start at the end of the hallway and work your way toward me so we can go faster!"

I ran back into their assigned room, yelling as I looked under the beds, in the closet, and anywhere else someone could hide. Once I realized no one was in the room I moved to the next. Three rooms down I paused as I heard something like voices. Frowning, I stopped to listen to what seemed like the end of the conversation. It sounded like a girl or a young child's voice but it was hard to hear clearly.

"Downstairs, the woman Ana. You'll be safe there. Yes. Quickly, go. We'll be right behind you." I heard Ruby say as I stepped out of the room.

I frowned, not seeing who she was talking to by the time I made it out of the room. "Did you find them? Where are they?"

Ruby jumped, almost as if I startled her. "It was the girl. She doesn't know where Liam is. I sent her on to the basement and said we'd keep looking."

My brow furrowed a little in confusion but I nodded. I did not take the time to process what she said past the fact Liam was missing. I turned, already moving back into search mode. "Okay. Let's keep looking. We need to hurry."

"She's already checked up here, apparently. Said she had been looking for him before she saw me."

A chill ran through me a little as I stopped from turning. "Really? Then where could he be?"

She shrugged and responded a little evasively. "I don't know but-"

"Wait-wait a second. She talked to you? She hasn't talked to anyone." I could have sworn I had heard voices, more than one. If she did randomly talk, that would explain why I was not sure who I was hearing.

Ruby glanced to the side and shrugged, "Uh, yeah. I guess maybe she did it because it was a serious situation. I don't know."

Confused again, I asked, "She said that much? You weren't talking that long were you?"

"Yeah, she did. Hey look, we need to get going if we are

going to find him. I have an idea of where to look. Come on!" She was gone before I could respond, running down the flight of stairs. "Come on, Ava! Hurry up!"

I shook my head but went after her. Things weren't making sense but it must have been the stress of the situation or something. My mind was running a million miles per hour. At least, that's what it felt like. Besides, now was not the time to be having conversations instead of trying to find Liam. He was only ten years old and was all alone with all of the chaos going on outside.

"Ruby! Wait!" I caught up to her when she was leaving the house. "We can't go out there! We need to be looking for Liam and then going to hide like Leo said."

Whipping around so fast her hair flew, Ruby answered my whispered complaint with her own. "I told you I had an idea where Liam could be. He has only lived up here at the house with you people for barely a week and it's not like you know what he spent his time doing before that. I do. Now, you can trust me, and let's go find him together, or I'll do it on my own."

My eyes widened and I took a step back in shock. Anger surged through me but I pushed it aside. "Listen, I don't appreciate your tone or the accusation behind it but that's not important right now. Let's hurry up and find Liam and get back. But you and I, we will be having a discussion about this later. I don't know what's gotten into you lately." I shook my head then pushed by her and went outside. "Let's go. Oh, and try not to be seen. The last thing we need is to be caught by whoever is doing all this."

I paused against the outside wall because I had just pushed by her in irritation and I was not going to admit she needed to be in the lead.

Ruby grumbled under her breath as she hurried past me. She led me around a smaller building that I was pretty sure was the outhouse and into the woods. I had seen it in the daytime, but everything on this side of the main house was dark so it was hard to see much. Then again, my eyes had not quite adjusted from stepping out of the lit house.

"Woah, Woah. Wait. What are you doing?" I hissed out in frustration when I realized where she was headed. The forest was basically on fire on the other side of the clearing and we were not supposed to even be outside of the house. There were still yells, and even some snarls, cutting through the chilly night air. We definitely should not be going into the dark woods.

Had she not seen *any* scary movie before?

"I told you I know where Liam used to play. Come on, it's only a couple hundred feet past that big tree there. I know what I'm doing. Let's go.

I rubbed my temple and looked back towards the house, torn. I had a bad feeling about being out here. But then I pictured Liam's face and huffed out a breath of air in frustration. I could not leave a little boy out here. No matter how weirded out I was feeling.

Sighing I said, "Fine, lead the way. But please hurry. I'm getting a bad feeling about this."

As we pushed through into the wooded tree line the little light we had from the outside torches and the fires disappeared, almost as if the night had swallowed them. Chill bumps spread down my arms just as a wolf's howl cut through the air. But I didn't even have time to contemplate the idea of turning back and insisting we look somewhere else. It was taking all of my concentration to try and keep up with Ruby's running form in front of me so I didn't lose her in the dark. The quicker we got through, the quicker we can get to Liam and get back.

I should have listened to my gut though. That tingle in my mind that had said something was wrong. The chills that had shot over my skin, and not because of the cold. But I didn't. I listened to Ruby.

I should have seen it coming.

One minute we were crashing through tree branches we couldn't see, branches and twigs scratching my skin as I stumbled to keep up. The next minute there were no trees. Ruby stopped so suddenly I bumped into her and stumbled.

Looking around, I frowned. "Is this it? There's nothing here. You said Liam was here, Ruby." We looked to be in a small natural clearing, but it was barely big enough for a few people to stand in. Nowhere near big enough for Liam to be here without us seeing.

Ruby turned and looked at me. It was so dark I could barely see her, but we were close enough to each other that I frowned at the strange look that I could have sworn crossed her face.

"No, Liam is not here, Ava."

Frowning more, I brushed my hands up and down my arms, trying to fight off the goosebumps as I took a step back.

"That's um, that's okay. It was a good idea. But now we're here and know he's not. So, let's get going. If we hurry, we can maybe find him before we absolutely need to get into safety." I took another step back.

Then I gasped as she lunged forward and grabbed my arms. Trying to shake her off I yelled, "What are you doing, Ruby. Let go!"

"No, I'm sorry. Ava. Liam was never here. I had to get you here. I'm sorry. But it's for your own good!"

Pushing her away, I stumbled back. "What do you mean never here? What are you talking about? Why would you waste our time when we're trying to find Li-." I gasped as I remembered the whispers I had heard in the house. I had thought it was weird that the girl who refused to speak or leave Liam would suddenly do both. But like a fool, I blinded myself to the facts. "You already found him! You found both of them in the house, didn't you?! Why would you lie?"

Ruby shook her head, "I really am sorry. But you can't see what has been right in front of you. You are brainwashed! I don't blame you. Truly. After the accident and learning everything we have, and you being kidnapped and auctioned off. Who wouldn't have a case of that- that syndrome people have.

What is it called? Oh! Stockholm Syndrome! Yes, it's for the best."

"What are you talking about?! I'm not brainwashed, Ruby! What is wrong with you?" I shook my head. "You know what, it doesn't matter. I don't know the purpose of all this, but it's done. I'm going back."

I turned around to push back through the trees I came through. I hoped I could get back quickly. Both to get inside and to be away from Ruby. I did not know what had gotten into her. I had thought maybe she had just needed time to cool down and realize she was wrong when she had yelled before. But I could see I had been wrong.

I had taken a few steps into the tree line, heading back in the direction we had come from when something suddenly fell from above and hit me in the head.

I groaned as I fell to the forest floor. I had not seen anyone before being hit and my head was already starting to pound. Through blurry eyes and a pounding headache, I tried to get up and see my attacker but I collapsed in pain.

Managing to look up, a blurry image of a cloaked figure was all I saw before the world went black.

CHAPTER SEVENTEEN

~Leo~

I hated being away from Ava; especially at a time like this.

After I left her in the house, despite everything inside of me snarling against the idea, I ran out to see what was going on. Frankly, it was simply more of a chaotic situation than a deadly one from what I could see.

Not that it did not have the potential to be deadly. Fires had been set on trees around the clearing which surrounded Gabriel's pack in what looked like an attempt to stop anyone from running. As of now, the fires had not spread to anywhere they couldn't be stopped or cause serious damage to. So, I did not think anyone could have been seriously burnt despite us hearing screams earlier. Though the darkness of the night added such a contrast to the brightness of the burning lights and the chill of the night air, a difference to the wall of blazing heat which was sure to conjure terrifying images in the minds of those who had been suddenly surrounded by it.

Screams and snarls were ringing out through the air even now, but I could tell the definitive difference from those I had heard early. Both had been screams of shock and fear, but these screams now were of pure, unadulterated terror. The sounds so chilling they brought goosebumps to my skin even though I knew none of the shifters would be doing anything to cause harm to the town's humans unless absolutely necessary, despite everything currently happening. In my opinion, despite their supposed good standing with this pack, the terror in those screams was a testament to how they really felt about the shifters.

Running, I assessed everything around me. I made sure no one needed help before turning to search for Gabriel.

There were humans from both the plane crash and the town sitting around; some scattered throughout the clearing in front of the packhouse while others were sitting near each other and talking. Some shifters were standing guard near the town's humans and clearing, clearly not willing to leave them alone. Some shifters were helping the human doctor from the plane crash as he made rounds to help people. I could see some people had burns, probably from getting too close to the fire. I was not an expert on fires or burns but I did not see any which looked deadly, but for sure would leave scarring. Still, there were many other shifters out in the darkness, tracking and capturing people, and helping others.

I looked around trying to see how many of the plane survivors were still missing but I did not know them well enough to know who was missing. A thought which made me feel ashamed. I could not have helped it, though. Not really. I was a shifter who had found a mate when I had genuinely not thought it would happen. I was an alpha whose unclaimed mate was surrounded by shifters; and not even those of my own pack.

As I was leaving to find Gabriel, my mind went back to Ava. She was basically the only constant on my mind since meeting her.

I could not recount the number of times I had looked for my mate before, only to be disappointed. Or the night's I ran my pack territory as a wolf, seeing all which my ancestors and I had built, and just knowing that I would have no one to share it with. The fear I faced daily about my future and that of the pack. We had all traveled so many times from place to place, just hoping that just one of us would find our mate. The only two times it had happened before, we knew each of us was simultaneously relieved and disappointed. Then the decision, despite the absolute disgust towards The Gathering and what it stood for, that we needed to expand our searches there. Even knowing that to do so would mean paying for our mate like she was an object if we were lucky enough to find her. Then I did.

That moment was one I would never forget.

The shifters who had been traveling with me and I walked into yet another auction. Having decided that we would visit just one more before heading back home for a break. Each of us is exhausted from endless running and mentally drained from endless let-downs. Then, amazingly, through the heavy stench of testosterone, sweat, and grime I smelled it. The natural scent was unique to everyone. Specifically, for a shifter, the scent was life, acceptance, and happening all rolled into one. My life had ceased to exist that day only to be immediately remade into a happier, better, and actual one. When I finally saw her, my whole world narrowed to where there was nothing but her and me. I felt happy, yes. But I also felt a peace and a purpose I had never felt before. At least, until the rage towards her treatment kicked in.

She became my life, my reason for living, that day. So, I really could not be faulted for wanting as much time as possible with her while we were here and I did not have the responsibility which would fall on me when I finally took her home.

When I finally tracked Gabriel down I saw him pacing in front of another group of humans, who I assumed were from town because they were surrounded by other shifters.

One thing's for sure, I thought to myself. *Whoever it is that caused all this didn't seem to mention to the town humans just how many shifters are currently visiting Alpha Gabriel's territory because they brought nowhere near enough people.*

I chuckled to myself when I realized I was thinking of him as Alpha Gabriel even in my head. I could hear the equally exasperated and amused response Ava would be sure to have.

"Who told you all this? What was bad enough that you would risk all of our lives and our relationship?"

Gabriel's voice snapped me out of my thoughts. Looking at the group of humans I watched each of them closely.

A misconception many people had was that the person who answered was always the one in charge. Sometimes they were and sometimes they weren't. Which was what made watching them all so important.

"I-I don't know where the conversation came from. I swear."

My gaze snapped to the owner of the voice briefly before moving on, watching the others. I had to remind myself this wasn't my territory and not my job to ask the questions. Even if I wanted to snarl at the idiots who risked harm to my mate and the people she cared for.

Clearly, Gabriel felt the same way because the snarled growl which erupted from deep in his throat was enough that the surrounding shifters stumbled a few steps, and they weren't even the ones being growled at. The only ones not physically freaked out by it were me and another visiting alpha who was standing with us. The humans had varying reactions but based on the quivering of some and the sudden stench of urine in the air I was pretty sure they were equally affected.

"You're saying you put the entire relationship of my pack and your town, the lives of everyone here and there, and hurt so many people for a reason you don't even know?!"

"N-n-no. We know the reason. Just not... who said it." The guy winced as he stammered. Hopefully realizing how stupid he sounded since he was admitting anyone could have started a rumor and they acted on it.

I glanced over at Gabriel to see his response and if he realized what I had also.

"Listen, we were just informed of these rumors of missing and kidnapped women that have been going around town. True or not, I admit it is concerning. But you hear a rumor, make connections which don't exist, and you decide to march on *my* territory and ruin *my* land and put *my mate* and my pack in danger?!" After Gabriel snarled that, the humans were basically curled on the ground in fear but the realization was beginning to seep into their eyes. "Nevertheless, I do understand your concerns. I am not ready to let this all go away with no repercussions but I won't let your stupidity jeopardize what the town leaders and I have all worked towards. In case you are certain yet, I'll allow you to talk to some of the human leaders amongst the group who live here. Just so we can settle this for all. They are not being held here against their will. After that, we *will* need to discuss this all and figure out just where this rumor came from. I won't be having this happen again."

Gabriel looked over at me, then the other alpha with us right now, and then nodded at the other shifters.

"Take them to the clearing and hold them all there. There are still some things which need to be done here. While you are all there, if you can ensure a smaller amount of shifters are able to keep watch on them, then those who aren't needed should help the others with the fires."

The shifters nodded, dipping their head in respect, then pulled the humans up from the ground to walk towards the packhouse.

I waited until they were gone before I said anything. "Are there more wandering around still?" Before he could answer me a couple more screams cut through the air.

I gave a dry, unamused chuckle. "I guess that answers that. What are we going to do with them? Trying to figure out who told them may not lead anywhere. This group, at least, really didn't know who."

Rubbing his temples and beginning to pace again, Gabriel nodded. "I agree those men didn't know anything but someone else here is bound to. We can't afford to not know who told them and the reason behind it. If there's an enemy in my territory I need to know before something like this happens again."

The other alpha finally spoke. I hadn't had the chance to meet him yet since he had just arrived so I didn't know his name. "I agree but it seemed like you were wanting to keep a decent standing with the town's people, so how will you get the answers out of them?"

Gabriel growled. "They put my mate in danger. I will do whatever I have to do. If they have an issue with it I will make it clear it was necessary and that it wouldn't have been had they not come here."

I grunted in acknowledgment. "I'm right there with you. My mate's here too and the fact something could have happened to her..." I closed my eyes and took a deep breath at the idea. "I've just found her. I can't lose her. I'll do anything I can to help you find out who's betrayed her. Because that's what this is."

Gabriel nodded and walked over to clasp him on the shoulder in a silent gesture of comradery. "Thank you. We'll make sure nothing happens to our women and none of the others."

Just then a howl split the air and we all looked up, heads tilting as we listened.

"Someone's found something. Let's go."

We all took off running, choosing not to shift since we knew we would be dealing with humans. Meaning, we would need our voices and humans tend to be distracted by the unavoidable nudity which accompanied shifting.

Arriving within 10 minutes, we found Silver and some other shifters surrounding the town's humans. Half of the shifters were still in their wolf forms. A human man was standing by Silver who I vaguely recognized as being one of the plane crash survivors. He looked to be in his late 20's or early 30's, solidly built with muscles obvious even under his clothing, around 6'4", and with a vicious look in his eye that seemed almost animalistic. The look a natural-born hunter and a warrior had; one a person normally had if he had seen and done a lot to protect himself and others. If he did not smell human I would believe he was a Shifter no questions asked. His power and authority radiated from him even as a human.

Looking at Silver, I nodded then darted a quick look to the human next to him and back. Asking Silver a silent question with the look which he seemed to pick up on.

Silver gave me a small nod and then cleared his throat. "Alphas. This is O'Conner of the plane humans. After realizing what was happening he helped save some people who had been on the other side or too close to the fire. When we noticed these men here running away, he came with us. Apparently, he's an excellent tracker." Silver threw a smirk in O'Connor's direction and teased him just briefly. "For a human."

Scoffing good naturally, O'Connor simply raised an eyebrow. "Not just a tracker but a fighter. I bet I could put you to the ground 30 seconds flat if you wanna spar later." Many of the shifters around us shot them an amused look.

Silver laughed. "Sure. Name the time and place. I promise to go easy on you."

Amused looks turned to small laughs. Their bantering offered a small sense of relaxation and humor before reality bled back in.

Getting serious, O'Connor turned to us. "Six months ago I was a soldier for our country's military. Now I'm a soldier without, I guess, something to be a soldier for. This was the most excitement I've had in a while so I was glad to help. Anyway, while they were hunting for everyone I caught these two hiding in some brush whispering."

He nodded towards the two he caught and then rolled his eyes.

"Idiots just laying there confessing all, completely unaware of their surroundings and like they weren't on the territory of people with wolf hearing."

The other humans with the group were shooting both confused and irritated looks at the two who knew more and had made it known they knew more.

Gabriel grunted, "What were they talking about?" His eyes narrowed on the two humans and slowly stalked towards them.

"Apparently they were the ones who were told this rumor directly and masterminded this wonderful example of misplaced stupidity."

Kneeling to stare them in the eyes. Though he was still talking to us, he snarled in their faces. "And just *who* told them that we somehow decided to turn against everything we believe in and manage to kidnap an entire group of humans?"

Silver cleared his throat, shooting a glance first to O'Connor then Gabriel. "Apparently it was a woman. But the idiots over there can't possibly tell you anything about how 'hot' she was."

Just like that, there were a lot of angered responses from everyone. Which I thought was ironic because in normal circumstances they would have probably been in the same boat.

"If they know she was hot then they know *something* about what she looked like. Or would at least recognize her again if they saw her." I cut in. "We know someone from here told them, right? So, if it comes down to it we can have them see women who may be the suspect."

Gabriel nodded. "Good idea." Then he talked directly to the men. "You're *going* to help us. Whether you want to or not. So, make it easy on everyone and tell us what you know."

The men nodded with wide, scared eyes. Both of them said yes at the same time.

Kneeling from a few feet away from where Gabriel and the men were, I looked at them. Trying to help encourage them I decided to try and help them remember. "Think about her. Was she taller than you? Or shorter? The same height? What was her hair like? Straight, curly, long, short? Was she a brunette or blond or something else? How about her build? You know what she looks like, you just have to remember and tell us."

The men took turns talking. Half talking to each other as they tried to remember and the other half saying things once they seemed to have either remembered or agreed on it.

The problem was that they were describing a person none of us had recalled seeing. Granted, that did not mean much when most of us standing here had spent too much time with the plane humans. But, someone who matched their description? We would have noticed. If I was not one-hundred percent sure they were too terrified to lie then I would have thought they were.

None of us had seen too many female shifters, but it sounded like they were describing one based on the few there had been over the years. Which made zero sense for many different reasons. One, a shifter would not have messed with a ton of packs due to possible fallback on their own pack. Not that we even had issues between packs these days. Why would we? There are plenty of territories to go around, a woman is either our mate or not, and traveling to different packs is basically non-existent. At least, it used to be. Two, we would have scented a shifter who did not belong anywhere near the territory; especially a female one. So, that could not have possibly been who told what was going on around here to these men.

I looked up and noticed Silver and Gabriel exchanging a knowing glance before Silver met my eyes.

None of this was making sense to any of us. But it especially was not sitting right with me. If these men were both telling the truth and remembering right, and I believed they were, then the person who started all this was very careful in covering their tracks. I did not like knowing that whoever orchestrated all of this was still out there and no closer to being caught. I knew the men agreed with me.

Growling in frustration, I ran a hand through my hair as I stood. "So, all we have is a description of a woman, who is not staying on your territory, with the knowledge that only someone who is staying on your territory can have! We're getting nowhere and whoever did all of this isn't any closer to being found. I don't like this. Isn't anyone else getting a bad feeling?"

The churning in the pit of my stomach made me feel like I was going to be sick. The raised flesh of goosebumps racing up my spine, over my neck, and down my arms made me feel restless. I really did not have a good feeling.

O'Connor finally spoke up after being silent the entire time we had been questioning the humans.

"Not necessarily. If this woman is not part of the groups here on the pack grounds, then the only other option is it's a town woman. Right? Otherwise, an unknown woman is walking around. I may be new here, but I kinda got the feeling that would be something someone would notice. Right?"

We all nodded.

"So, whoever *did* somehow manage to sneak out of here, into town, and back most likely told the woman these men are talking about. So, all we have to do is find the woman who told *them*, and then we can get her to help us find the person who told *her*."

Nodding, Gabriel finally stood from his place in front of the line of humans.

"Yes, but do we really have time for all of that? I mean, look at all that's happened here. By the time we get them all taken care of, get into town, and find her we may have lost our shot. Or maybe another attack is on the way."

I shook my head. "Doubt it. These people who told them everything to get them to do all this were simply instigators. They weren't doing any of it to plan attacks or attack themselves. But whatever we do, we need to do it fast. My wolf is getting really agitated and restless, and I really need to get back to Ava."

My head snapped to the left as I suddenly heard running headed in our direction and fast.

I turned to face the potential threat just as they cleared the trees and then relaxed a fraction once I realized it was one of the wolves sent to the house to check on Ava, Ana, and the others.

The look on his face stopped me as tingles erupted over my skin, my heartbeat picking up in my chest, and adrenaline beginning to pump through my veins.

"What's wrong?" I growled, scared something bad happened. I *had* been having a bad feeling for the past few minutes when we were trying to figure out the traitor amongst us, knowing they could be anyone. Now, I knew I was right. Something bad had happened and I had left Ava alone.

With that thought, my eyes probably flashed gold as the anger coursing through my body began to weaken the handle I had on my wolf. Demanding to be set free, find our mate, and kill whoever had endangered her. I was already in the motion of running past him when his words stopped me cold.

"Luna Ava and the woman Ruby never made it to the basement safe room. By the time we went looking, no one had seen them or could find them."

The pain, fear, and anger coursing through my body shredded my control and I shifted. My clothes practically disintegrated at the speed of my shift. I took off running as fast as I could towards the packhouse, knowing she wasn't there but I could maybe catch her trail. As I did so, I threw my head back and howled, letting all of the pain and rage I felt bleed through into the night air.

Let them hear. Whoever there are, let them hear and know I am coming for them. They will regret taking what's mine.

CHAPTER EIGHTEEN

My head was pounding so hard I could swear there was ringing in my ears. I groaned in pain as I shifted a little to try and raise my head. Quickly I stopped as the pain increased, sending sharp slashes of bone-aching pain throughout my body. Obviously, that was not a smart thing to do. I tried to open my eyes next.

Oh, geez. I must have lost some brain cells because why do I keep moving? I thought to myself as pain once again shot through me.

Simply cracking my eyes resulted in my head protesting the movement and all for nothing. I could not see anything at all. At the realization panic shot through me. Where was I? What happened? Why couldn't I see?

Slowly, I began to remember. Ruby snapping, or was it not snapping when she had just lost her mind? Following her into the woods and straight into a trap. Something hitting me.

Whoever was with Ruby probably was right next to me. Which meant I had already, inadvertently, let them know I was awake. Since I could not see or lift my head with pain shooting through it, I strained to listen. Attempting to hear anything that could help me. Who was working with Ruby? Did I know them? How many were here? Were they saying anything I could use against them or let me know what I was dealing with?

There was nothing but silence.

As panic once more filled my body, I tried to remain calm. My mind immediately went to Leo. Was he still helping with whoever had seemingly attacked the pack? Was he okay? I had to believe he was. Mates and everything about them passed all laws of nature, as I knew them. Or used to know them. I was sure I would know if something bad had happened to him, whether we were fully mated or not. Was he out there looking for me right now? Did he even know I was missing yet? As panic began to seep back in at my inability to suppress it, I was also filled with regret. Regret I had continued to hold him at arm's length where anything mating was concerned. Regret I had been thinking more with my head than with my heart.

I realized it was all based on a place filled with uncertainty and fear; of the unknown and our differences. But what if he never finds me? What if I never escape whatever situation I am in and find my way back to him? The idea I would never have a relationship and life with my soulmate because of my own insecurities was something truly worthy to panic about.

I banished that thought. *No. I'm not going to think like that. Think of a way to get out. What did my research for my one book and all of those crime show reruns teach me? When you're kidnapped you need to assess the situation. Figure out your surroundings, your kidnappers, their motivation. Think like that and when I get back to Leo, I will make sure I don't hold myself back any longer.*

With that motivating thought, I tried to open my eyes once more. At first, everything was still black and a small amount of panic came filtering back in. Was I blindfolded? Was I *blind*? Then I relaxed when I finally began to see a few things as my eyes adjusted and some of the blurriness I was experiencing faded away. My eyes were just a bit blurry from being hit and it was still dark. No wonder I had only seen black.

From the corner of my eye, I saw movement; just barely noticeable in the pitch-black of the night with the forest blocking any potential light.

My head whipped around to figure out what I saw and then I groaned. I had already forgotten about my head. Ignoring it as best I could, I tried to focus on the spot I had seen movement; willing myself to see. There was a shape I could not distinguish, other than knowing it was a person sitting on the ground watching me. I could not see their face to know their eyes were watching me but I could feel it just as certainly as any prey feeling the eyes of a predator on them. Chills spread across my body.

I waited, expecting the person to do something or say something. When minutes went by without any change, I decided to say something. I had watched many crime shows in my life, both based on reality and fiction. I knew each kidnapper or killer had different things which set them off; different things which you could appeal to them with. I was not sure how to approach a situation where I did not know who had kidnapped me or why. But I knew I was not going to sit here and wait around to see what was in store for me. Shifting my position slowly, so as not to make the pain in my head flare up anymore and not to make the person nervous, I sat up and realized I was not even tied up. Shocked, I lifted my head to watch the shape of the person. What kind of kidnapper kept their victim in the forest and did not tie them up? I shuddered to think of the answer.

After another few minutes of silence, I broke. I wanted answers and the silence was freaking me out as much as the situation.

"Um, hi. Who are you?" I internally cringed at myself. *Great! Now I'm like one of those stupid people who know someone's in their house and asks who's there!*

The shape of what I assumed was the person's head tilted to the side a little. I frowned. It kind of reminded me of what the shifters around the territory do when they are curious about something. Was this person a shifter? If so, why would they be working against other shifters and with Ruby who has made it very obvious she doesn't trust them?

Could it be this person wasn't with Ruby and whoever had knocked me out and had instead saved me? It would explain why I was not tied up. The excitement began to grow inside me as I began to hope. Just as quickly, though, it departed. If that was the case, then why was I still in the forest and why was the person both hiding and not talking to me?

This entire situation was making me equally more confused and more nervous. Nothing made sense.

"Are you the person who knocked me out? Why? What do you want?"

Still nothing. I was growing frustrated.

"Where's Ruby?" I looked around but could not see anyone else. Then again, it was dark. The only reason I could see this person's shadow, whoever they were, was the moonlight barely breaking through the cover of the trees.

The shadowed person moved forward just a little, but enough for me to see they wore a black cloak with the hood pulled up. Then the hood was pushed back and my eyes widened.

The person was a woman, a shifter woman. Now that her hood was pushed back I had seen her eyes glow for a second. What was even more shocking, and unsettling, was that her wolf's eyes were not golden like Leo's were but were a soft red. Almost pink. Then the glowing stopped and I focused on the rest of her. She was beautiful from the little I could see of her. Which made sense, I guess, seeing how all of the male shifters I knew were insanely attractive in their own ways. She had dark hair that was pulled back so I could not tell much about it in the dark. She was toned and tall, the latter I was assuming since she sat higher than me. Her facial features, from what I managed to see in the little light I had, were striking. Her jawline prominent, lips full, cheekbones high, and nose straight. I could not see what her normal eyes looked like, but I was sure they were equally as striking.

"You're a shifter!" I said incredulously. "I haven't seen a female shifter before! I heard you guys were very rare and none of them have come yet. Have you come with the new pack that arrived today?"

I scooted forward a little, both intrigued and sure I was safe. Since she was a shifter had to have saved me. Maybe she simply did not know how to get back to the pack since she just got here. Or waited until I was awake because she couldn't carry me and did not want to leave me.

Another head tilt and the woman's brow furrowed a little. "You know a lot of shifters. How?"

Confusion filled me. "Well, my mate is a shifter. An alpha to be exact. Besides, when he found me all of the packs were so excited they answered any questions I have."

"Really?" She seemed shocked.

I nodded, my confusion growing. "Of course." My answer was drawn out, feeling like it should have been obvious.

"And you... trust them?"

I sat back as I frowned. "Well, yea. They saved me and the others."

"Others?"

"Yea... others. You know the rest of the plane crash survivors?"

There seemed to be no recognition on her face. If anything, there seemed to only be more confusion. A strange feeling spread through me as I began to second guess myself. If she was with any of the packs she should have known about all of this.

"You're not with any of the packs are you?" I asked slowly; hesitantly.

The woman shook her head in answer, still watching her in a predatory or analytical way.

"Then who are you? What do you want from me?"

Ignoring my answers, she spoke again. "You trust the people

who bought you like you were no better than a cow? Who basically kidnapped you?"

She knew about that but not about the reason why I was a victim of The Gathering in the first place. She did not know about where I came from or the other people. So, where was she getting her information?

Ruby. My eyes widened as it dawned on me. I had not been wrong that someone had been working with Ruby. That someone else had knocked me out.

"Why are you doing this? I'm assuming Ruby told you about The Gathering. About me being kidnapped and bought. But she didn't tell you all the facts. I think you know that. So why would you decide to kidnap me yourself?"

She winced and looked away. "I don't think of it as kidnapping. I'm setting you all free. The Gathering has gone on too long. No one stops it. Now, shifters are even encouraging them. Visiting and buying people."

"But you know shifters have mates. That with how much it costs, they would only buy their mates. And only so they could rescue them. No other reason. You're a shifter, so you have to know that."

She shook her head and snarled, "It doesn't matter! There will be no end to it! No end if no one takes a stand. I'm rescuing people. Giving them an actual chance at life. No one else is!"

My eyes widened as I remembered them saying the rumors going through town about women disappearing around the country. Women who had been a part of The Gathering.

"It's you! You've been kidnapping or rescuing or whatever you want to call it, women across the country! You're the reason behind the attack on the pack territory!"

CHAPTER NINETEEN

I broke through the tree line running as fast as I could, leaving the clearing we had been standing in. My vision narrowed, tunneling in my single purpose of getting my mate back. So, I was not paying attention to my surroundings.

Before I could get a few feet into the trees a heavy force of another shifter's wolf slammed into my side. I snarled in anger even as my body flew sideways through the air, only stopping once it slammed into a tree.

My wolf's feet scrambled to get purchase underneath my body so I could shove at the other wolf who landed on top of me.

With a forceful shove of four paws, I launched the other wolf across the clearing. My mind narrowed and my vision faded into tunnel vision as anger coursed through me. Anger at whoever dared stop me from going to save my mate, no matter who they were.

As the other wolf landed and spun around to face me, growling in warning with his hackles raised I saw something in the corner of my eye. Someone else was here.

I snarled, stepping to the side to try and keep both the threats in my line of sight. Vaguely I realized the newcomer, Silver, was still in his human form. But I knew it did not make him any less dangerous.

Tilting my head towards the wolf, I allowed myself a moment to inhale. Scenting the air I realized the wolf was Gabriel. This served to confuse me and anger me all at the same time.

How dare another alpha attack me and keep me from rescuing my mate. The only way so many alphas and packs can be here is we all respect each other. But here he was not respecting me. *I doubt he would have done anything differently if it was his mate who was missing.*

Just that thought made me snarl at them again, taking a step forward with my teeth bared in anger.

"Wait! Wait-wait-wait." My head swung back towards Silver, baring my teeth at him in a warning.

So far he had not done anything to anger me, but he was not very far from it.

"Leo... Alpha Leo. Calm down. We aren't trying to keep you from finding her. But... please shift back. Both of you. I'm tired of being the one talking to fangs."

My nose scrunched up to show said fangs but I huffed out in irritation. I could not afford to wait on finding Ava. But, now that I was not seething in anger, I realized they may have a point in stopping me.

With the smoke from the fires, I would not be able to catch her scent and I did not know his territory very well.

Snarling one more time I shifted back to my, now naked, human form. Once Gabriel shifted, I spoke in a clipped voice. Still angry but willing to hear them out. As long as it was quick.

"What was so important that not only am I wasting precious time, but you have the audacity to attack me."

Gabriel winced and rubbed a hand through his hair. His southern accent was stronger than I had ever heard it. "Attack is a little... strong. But I'm sorry about that Alpha. We just needed to stop you before..."

"Before what? What is more important than my Ava?!" My voice raised at the end in a growl.

Gabriel glanced at Silver with a pained look on his face. A look, I suspected, was more about angering me further than it was about what they had to say to me.

Silver's dry tone answered me. "Look, as much as I just *love* having important conversations with naked men while knowing any second it can blow up right in front of me, this is important. You need to hear us. Not just listen, but hear what we are trying to tell you."

"All he told us was that Ava and Ruby hadn't been seen in a while. We don't know where they are or if they're even together! So you can't just run off. You need to think about this clearly."

I sighed in disappointment. Gabriel was right. They both were. "But I can't just sit around here doing nothing! You're right, we don't know what's going on. But that doesn't mean she's safe. She could be out there needing help!"

"Yes, I'm not arguing. But she could also be still in the house for all we know. We need to plan. Ask around."

Silver nodded and agreed with Gabriel. "You know I care for Ava too. Come on, not like that." He said in exasperation when I growled. "I'm just saying, I will... no, we will help you find her. No matter what's happened. But not only do we need to plan if it comes to it, but we also shouldn't rush into things without finding the facts."

"You'll all help me find her? Now? I understand what you're both saying and I'll try to wait as long as I can. But I have a bad feeling about this. I had one earlier and didn't realize it. I can't wait here a moment more."

Just then the human from earlier, O'Connor stepped from the tree line silently. I glanced over, startled. I had not heard him coming. Glancing at the others, I wondered if they heard him but they looked just as startled.

"Don't mind me. Took a while to catch up but I'm glad I did. After you three left someone came. They found Ruby. She's in the main clearing."

My eyes widened and I started to turn to run there when his voice stopped me.

"Just Ruby. Not Ava."

I turned back towards him. "What do you mean, not Ava. They were together. They shouldn't be separated."

"Well, that's just it. Ruby said they split up to cover more ground when they were searching for the kids. She says she took the house and Ava insisted on looking outside."

Frowning, I shook my head. "No, that can't be right. I told her to look upstairs. I saw her go upstairs. And she knew better than to go outside."

"Well, that's what Ruby said. But I'm not sure I believed her. She... she was acting very twitchy."

"Twitchy?" Gabriel asked and crossed his arms.

"Yea, she couldn't really meet my eyes for any length of time and kept licking her lips. I don't exactly know what you guys do to tell lies, sniff each other's butts? But, I know someone who's lying or making something up when I see one."

Silver barked out a laugh. "Sniff each other's butts. Yea sure. Says the human. You wish you were as cool as us."

Gabriel and I growled at the same time, silently telling him to be serious.

"So, what are you saying? Ruby knows where my mate is and is lying about it? Why would she do that?"

"Remember how adamant she was about how we weren't to be trusted?" Gabriel reminded me. "Maybe she still thinks that?"

"Or maybe she just was nervous by O'Connor's dazzling smile over there and that's why she was acting nervous."

I snarled at the same time O'Connor grinned at Silver and flipped him off. "Stop it! Please. I'm barely holding on by a thread and I'd hate to find my mate only to tell her that I murdered her taco maker because he was testing my patience."

Silver's hands flew up into the air, surrendering even though I saw him and O'Connor flash one last grin at each other.

Looking at the human warrior I asked, "So, could what he have suggested be true? That there was another reason why she was acting nervous?"

He shook his head. "No. I mean there *could* technically be another reason. But I really don't think so. She was agitated, kept looking around and towards the woods like she was expecting something to happen. Most likely, it was what Gabriel suggested. Sorry. Alpha Gabriel." He shook his head a little; I'm assuming at correcting himself since Ava didn't like saying titles either.

"But if she was lying, even if it was because she didn't think we could be trusted... how would she have convinced Ava to leave? And why would she put her friend in danger? At least, that's how Ava sees her."

I glared at Silver for him talking about Ava casually. But I shook my head. Now was not the time. Besides, I had to keep reminding myself not to kill him. *Ava, Mine, would really not like that.*

Despite not liking how he talked about my mate, I did agree with him. "He's right. I don't think she would do something to hurt Ava."

Gabriel nodded slowly, looking like his mind was miles away. "No, I agree. But what if she convinced Luna Ava, some-how, to leave with Ruby herself believing she was saving her. What if she knew she wasn't putting her in danger..."

Confusion filled me at first. What Gabriel said was not making sense. What would be so important that Ava left during an attack and how would Ruby know it was fine to do so.

My eyes widened as realization dawned at the same time O'Connor spoke up, nodding his head.

"I had the same thought. We know someone here told some mysterious person about us. And that mystery person told the town's people. We were having a hard time finding out who would be able to get that close to the territory undetected, or get out and back in unnoticed... but after her blow up everyone gave Ruby her space. No one messed with her, hoping she just needed some more time."

"It makes sense... she had the opportunity to leave without anyone realizing and if she was the one who told that woman in town then she also would know it would be safe to convince Ava to leave the main house." Silver agreed, serious once more.

I growled out in anger and frustration. "So, it's probably her who started all this. But that doesn't answer where my mate is."

Gabriel nodded. Straightening up from the tree he had been resting against he spoke up once more. "Okay. You go search the forest in the north. Silver, search the south. I'll go back to the house and have a talk with Ruby to see if she'll talk. Try and get her to tell me where your mate is."

"What about me? I can help."

Wincing, Gabriel looked over at him. "Sorry. I'll have other shifters scouring the East and West parts of the forest but we can't afford to have you slowing them down. You can come with me to talk to Ruby. Or help the others in the main clearing."

O'Connor shook his head. "Listen, I know I'm just some human to you guys but that doesn't mean I don't know what I'm doing. I know none of you heard me arrive. That wasn't because you all were talking when I showed up. I know how to hunt. More specifically, I know how to hunt humans. It was kind of my job. So, I can help. But I will go back with you before I go out. They can go ahead and start searching and I'll go when I've scouted exit points from the main house."

"Exit points?"

"Yea. We know Ruby and Ava, presumably, both escaped the main house without anyone seeing."

We all gave him a confused look. But I also had irritation beginning to course through my body with the undeniable feeling that I was wasting time.

"With how many shifters and humans all running around

outside and at least one human woman left the biggest, most central building in the territory unseen? If I can find out how, and where the main house hides from the view of everything else, I can maybe figure out which direction she went into the forest if she is in the forest."

My eyes widened. "Yes, please do that. Now, can I go look for my mate? Or will I be slammed into a tree again?"

I glanced at Gabriel with narrowed eyes.

He grimaced and nodded. Stepping to the side he jerked his head. "Go, the two of you. I'll send shifters to the other sections. Find your mate."

With that, for the second time in what seemed like the longest day of my life, I shifted to my wolf form and ran.

CHAPTER TWENTY

My eyes widened as I remembered them saying the rumors going through town about women disappearing around the country. Women who had been a part of The Gathering.

"It's you! You've been kidnapping or rescuing or whatever you want to call it, women across the country! You're the reason behind the attack on the pack territory!"

"I needed to do something! You should understand better than anyone!"

"I do! But that doesn't mean you stoop to their level and go around kidnapping people! Or convincing a bunch of men to go attack innocent people!"

She winced a little.

"Do you even ask the women you take if they need saving? If they want to leave? Have you ever thought, bought at auction or not, they may enjoy who they're with now?"

"Of course I do! I only rescue those who need it!"

An unamused laugh came out of me in a huff. "Yeah? So, why did you have Ruby lure me out into the woods during an attack which you created? Why did you knock me out and kidnap me? I didn't need saving. I don't need saving. I agree The Gathering was awful. Crazy. It needs to be stopped. But I learned very quickly, Leo... these shifters... are not my enemy. This is where I belong now. But *you* kidnapped me. You've taken the first step those people who kidnap for The Gathering have. If you don't have any standards to hold yourself to then you'll end up no better than they are!"

"I do have standards! I admit I regret allowing myself to ignore the fact I wasn't getting all of the information. I'll never do that again. But I've seen what The Gathering does to people! You can be so relieved you're being rescued that you blind your-self to the reality of the situation!"

"That will only happen if you allow that to happen! I can promise you, I have not been fooled by some misguided notion of heroism. I'm clear-minded. If anyone is having difficulty looking past their notion of truth to not pay attention to what's really going on, it's Ruby. And just maybe you, also. Do you even know there are roughly 40 humans who are living in this pack territory and are perfectly content and safe? Legitimately rescued by the shifters. Yet, you just sent men in to attack them all. Men who set fire to the forest, endangering everyone there. For what? Your personal vendetta?"

I was beginning to think this woman herself had a specific reason behind her hatred of The Gathering. A personal one. Which would make what she was doing understandable. The way she was doing it, though? Not so much.

"For that, I'm sorry. As I said, my information was wrong. I was unaware of... really, everything."

After saying that she fell silent.

"What exactly did Ruby tell you?"

She shrugged. "She told me about you, how you were kidnapped and auctioned off at The Gathering. How you were bought by a pack of wolves. How you and a group of humans were all being held against your will by the pack. Said you were blinded by the fact they saved you. Didn't see what was right in front of your minds."

"And she didn't tell you any specifics? Like where we all came from, and how they genuinely saved us?"

The woman shook her head. So, I told her. Everything from getting on the plane, to crashing, being sent out for help and being kidnapped, to being rescued and finding a new home.

"Ruby... she's young. And scared. She doesn't really under-stand just how much the pack, all of the packs, have done for us. She just sees the fact she's now in a world she doesn't know and away from all she's known. I don't think she's truly accepted the fact there is no going back and the fact she's not alone. She just feels like she is because the rest of us have, for the most part, come to terms with our new realities."

She growled softly. "I wish I had realized she was just a girl who was going through something. I let my anger get the best of me. Allowed me to ignore things I should have picked up on. Things I normally pick up on."

After a few moments of silence, I spoke again. "So, what now?

"Well, do you really want to stay here? It doesn't matter if he's your mate or if they saved you if you don't want to stay. I'll help you leave."

I sat back with a smile as I pictured the face of Leo; how he made me feel. I fully believed him when he told me how he felt, how much I meant to him, and how lucky he felt to have had his mate be me. I knew what finding his mate, finding me, gave him. It was not a lie or an over-exaggeration. After the time it took me to decompress from the overwhelming feelings I had when I first got here, I have come to realize how I genuinely had grown to care about Leo too. Maybe even love him. He saved me and he loved me without pressuring me to return his feelings in any way. Even though I knew it was literally in his DNA to claim me immediately.

So, I told the woman that.

"I understand your concerns or what it may look like, but I

really am happy with Leo. He saved me in more ways than one. You know, I never expected to get onto a plane and then survive a plane crash, and I did. I never expected to time travel into the future, or get kidnapped, or auctioned off, and I did. I never expected to learn shifters were real or that I was a shifter mate, but all of that happened. Yet, even before I got on the plane I was never truly happy. I was always striving towards something that was never in reach. I needed saving then, just not knowing it... and I needed saving after I got here. But the only thing is, with Leo, he's always saving me. Even with the simplest things like making sure I eat or making sure I have a moment of peace if I need it. And I know he'd save anyone because that's just the kind of guy he is, but he goes the extra mile with me because he loves me. I... I love him." I finished, saying the last part in a wonder-filled tone.

My eyes widened as I finally realized the truth. Before it had been a possibility I thought of with hope and uncertainty. Now I knew it was the truth. I loved Leo.

I shook my head to clear it. "As you can see, I don't need rescuing."

The woman settled back with a faint smile on her lips. "It sounds like you two are true mates. I *am* sorry for all this. I see now I made a mistake with all of this."

I shake my head. "Don't worry about it. I really do realize you had good intentions. If not a little misguided. I partially blame myself for that, I'm not gonna lie. I really thought Ruby was just upset and needed time to just... relax. I never imagined she'd take it so far."

Her head tilted back and forth. "Sometimes we can only realize our mistake when we've done something drastic enough to make us realize. So, what will you do now? Will you go back and have her punished?"

My eyes widened. "No! Of course, not. I still believe she was just misguided and upset. I won't necessarily be trusting her to be on her own or learn important things for a while, but I don't want her gone. I hope she knows that. Speaking of which, where is she?"

"She left after I knocked you out. Said she had to make sure no one got hurt." The woman winced. "Sorry about that, again."

I winced also, still feeling the pain in my head but brushed it off. Then I motioned that it was fine.

"You can come too, you know? I'm still amazed none of them have mentioned a female shifter without a pack. I'm assuming you don't have a pack, right?"

She nodded. "I lost my pack a long time ago. So, no. It's the very reason why they didn't mention me. They don't know I exist. And I thank you, but no... I can't give up on this mission. I need to see it through and I need a certain level of secrecy to do it. I can't have people knowing what I am or what I look like."

"They don't believe in The Gathering either! They wouldn't jeopardize you. And they'd be so excited to learn about another female shifter. I mean, what about your mate? I'm sure you have one and who knows how long he's simply been in a pack, waiting."

"One day, I may want to meet my family. But, honestly, I can't think of that. Not until I've saved every single woman I could. Not until The Gathering is finished. It's the promise I made myself many years ago, and the promise I'll keep."

"But who knows how long that'll take! You'd really risk the possibility of never finding an actual life? Because right now it seems like you're just finding a reason to survive. To me, it doesn't seem like you're really living. Doesn't it get lonely?"

She shrugged but glanced away. "That's the path I've chosen to take. Anyway, I'm truly sorry for the misunderstanding and this entire situation. You can go now. It's in that direction and if you get lost, I'm sure it won't be for long. I heard a howl right before you woke up. I'm sure it was your mate and he won't be far now."

She stood up and offered her hand to me. Taking her hand, I stood as well.

"Be free. If you decide to tell them about me, I'll understand. I just ask you to keep my mission, what I do, and what I look like a secret as much as you can."

"You really won't come with me?"

She shook her head. "No. Be well, Ava. Be happy."

The woman lifted her hood back up, turning to fade into the dark.

"Wait! You never even told me your name!"

She chuckled softly and smiled back at me softly. "One day, my mission will be finished. Hopefully, we meet again and then I'll tell you. Goodbye, Luna."

Then she disappeared into the night, the darkness swallowing her.

Turning in the direction the woman had told me to go, I shook my head in bewilderment from the entire situation that had just happened. Then I began to head back towards my new home. Home being Leo and not Gabriel's pack. I cannot believe I just now realized how I felt about Leo, and the first person I told was my kidnapper. I chuckled dryly to myself. I would not wait any longer. As soon as I found Leo I would tell him.

First, I just had to find my way through the forest in the dark. After I found Leo and finally told him how I felt, I would find Ruby. I would not hold anything that happened here against her. But she would have a long road to get back to normal.

CHAPTER TWENTY-ONE

"If the forest has a day of fire and the heat of the flames does not consume a special tree, it will still be changed; charred, but still standing."
 - Dan Groat

As I stumbled through the forest in the dark, I continued to hope I was going the right way.

Branches kept hitting me everywhere my skin was exposed; my face and my arms even more so. I just knew I was going to end up looking like someone used my body as a cat's scratching post or a human pin cushion. But it could not be helped. I could not see anything.

Great. Just my luck. The first time I'm about to confess my love to someone and I'll look like someone tried to murder me with paper and leaves.

It was all I could do to keep rubbing my hands along the tree bark to try and keep walking in a straight line. Even though I could feel the bark digging into my palms, tearing at the skin that had begun to go numb from the cold night air.

They said when you take away one of the senses, in my case my ability to see in the dark, that the other senses become stronger. I began to question if I believed that as I stumbled through the black of night, continuing to trip on tree roots and scratch myself on branches.

Just then I tripped over a raised tree root and caught myself on a tree branch with nothing but my hair.

I could not control the pain-filled scream which ripped from my throat as my full body weight, assisted by gravity, went hurtling to the ground while my hair was firmly stuck on whatever it was caught on. My scalp practically screamed just as loud as I did. My hands flew up to grab the base of my hair, where it met my scalp, to try to release pressure on my head and keep my hair from ripping out.

What did I do to deserve this?! I screamed in my mind. I mean, really. I had never had so much bad luck in my life as I seemed to be having recently.

As I managed to get my body pulled up under me so I could stand, I started the tedious task of untangling my increasingly frizzy hair from my sweat, in the dark. It was a process because my curly hair naturally tangled itself badly, but now it had dirt, leaves, and blood caked into it as well. The entire time I tried to untangle my hair enough to get it off the branch I mumbled aloud to myself in frustration. If someone was watching me they would probably think I was crazy.

"What did I ever do to have this much bad luck?"

"'Take a trip on a plane,' they said. 'It'll be fun,' they said."

"Then I get the *wonderful* opportunity of being kidnapped. Not once, but twice! Three times if you consider being bought against my will. Then again, I felt like I would have chosen my buyers over the sellers."

My chuckle was a bit deranged at the thought, I'm sure. Especially considering one of the said buyers was, as I now knew him, my mate. I shook my head a little, shivered at the cold that was getting worse now that I had stopped moving, and continued talking.

"Now look at me... in the dark, in the woods, bleeding, with my head stuck on a tree."

I sighed and blinked away the tears threatening to fall from irritation and from the pain my entire body was now in. After ranting for what seemed like ages, I finally managed to get all of my hair free from the branch. From what I could tell, at least.

Sighing, I brushed my hands against my pant legs, stood up straight, and smiled. No pain. That must mean I got it all. Taking a step forward, I once more felt my body topple forward. Simultaneously I felt the sharp sting from a few strands of hair being torn from my head and my ankles hitting a hard thing sticking out of the ground. My eyes filled with water at the small burn on my scalp even as I scrambled to catch my falling body. My body did not stop once it hit the ground and instead continued to roll with me both yelling and grunting along for the ride. When my body finally stopped, it was aided by slamming into a gigantic tree trunk.

I groaned in pain as I laid there against the tree. There was now no place on my body untouched by the intense hurt I now had coursing inside. I could feel my muscles starting to bruise and I didn't even want to think about it. Those were the worst because they took the longest to heal, hurt the worst, and you never even saw them until days later.

Eyes closed, I took a deep breath and realized that not only did I probably get tripped by the same tree root that had gotten me the first time, I also clearly did not manage to get all of my hair untangled from the branch.

Slowly I raised my hand to my head, groaning at the movement. Every shift caused sharp pain in my stiff, aching muscles and a feeling of tingling running through me that felt just like those you got when a body part fell asleep. Despite how much it ached to move, though, part of me needed to make sure I did not have a bald spot. *Call me superficial but there's only so much a girl could take.*

After learning I somehow had lucked out in one area at least,

I sighed in relief. Which reminded me of every other part of my body. I groaned and rested my head against the tree bark that my body was wrapped around like it was a pole I was trying to climb.

It hurt so much to breathe, let alone move, but I needed to get up. Lest I end up staying here throughout the night and being eaten by whatever other predator was stalking through the woods.

That would be just par for the course now, I guess.

Taking a few points to breathe deep and give myself a pep talk, I nodded to myself. Then I pushed up off the forest floor with a groan from moving my body and from the fact I found pine cones to use as a placemat for my hands. Forcing myself up, I took a moment to lean against the tree. A tear slipped from my eye, probably leaving a streak through the grime undoubtedly covering my face. I brushed it off in defiance and said aloud, "Show no fear Ava. You're almost there. Keep it together just a little while longer."

What fear I wasn't showing? I didn't know. At this point I was just saying whatever I needed to say to not completely fall apart; apparently using the nickname Leo's Beta gave me even in my head now.

Nodding to myself I pushed off the tree with a grunt, using my body to do so since my arms were beginning to feel like noodles. Then I began to shuffle forward, hoping the direction I was going in was still right.

After who knows how long, but probably only a few minutes later, I began to see a light.

Just like that, adrenaline shot through my body, giving me another wave of energy to go with my excitement. *I must be close to the pack!*

Beginning to half shuffle, half stumble forward faster, I felt the smile on my face growing and hope fluttering in my chest. Until I broke through a set of trees.

I could see the light just ahead and, of course, that's when I tripped over a vine of a root. I wasn't sure but I guess it didn't really matter. In my gaining pursuit of freedom, I failed to pay attention to my surroundings. A lesson I thought I had just learned but apparently had not.

My body once more went flying through the air. Like a punch to the chest, my breath and the excitement I just had were ripped from me. As I laid there, I managed to roll over onto my back but it took everything I had. So much so, that I felt the energy practically draining from my limbs with each moment. I was so tired. Laying there, as each second passed and I listened to crickets chirping in the night, I grew more tired and colder. Staring up into the blackness, I wondered if it wouldn't be too bad to just lay there and take a quick nap. Just long enough to be able to get more energy to move again.

Despite knowing it was a dumb idea, my body began to shut down anyway.

As my eyes began to close a rustling from the trees startled me. My eyes flew open and I looked in the direction from which it came. I realized it was the same direction the light had been in. In fact, the light was getting closer.

Renewed hope surged through me and gave me the power to raise my head and yell for help. "Hello! Who's there? Can you help me?"

There was some more rustling and then the person with the light came towards me.

My whole body sighed in relief and my head fell back to the ground. "Thank you for coming." My eyes closed in silent thanks and exhaustion. "I was worried I'd never get out of these woods."

Looking back at the person, I frowned at them still holding the light in front of their face.

"I'm afraid I can barely move right now. It's weird like all my energy has been zapped. If you can just give me a few moments I should be able to and then we can be on our way."

The person walked towards me and knelt at my side, finally

lowering the lantern to the ground at the same time she spoke. "Are you okay? Why can't you move? What *happened* to you?"

In shock, I stared at her. Then anger filled me. Fisting my hands into the dirt at my side, I struggled to a semi-reclined position. I didn't want to be laying down with her above me and completely useless. Through narrowed eyes, I stared at her and responded through gritted teeth. "You should know. You're the reason I'm out here in the first place."

Ruby cringed back and her eyes darted from side to side before settling on my forehead, not meeting my eyes. "I'm so sorry! I know I shouldn't have but I just... I can't stand how everyone takes this life and what we are told at face value! Especially you, Ava! You weren't meant to be hurt, just rescued."

"Face value? Especially me? What the heck are you talking about?!" I yelled, staring at her with wide eyes. "I didn't need rescuing. I needed to not be lied to and knocked out! You aren't making sense!"

"You were supposed to be my friend! And you've all but abandoned me, listening to their half-truths!"

"Half-truths? I'm really not understanding what you're goin' on about Ruby!" My voice raised, and my accent deepened a little, in exasperation. Which served just to make me more irritated, if I was honest with myself. I hated the southern accent I had and couldn't seem to shake no matter how hard I tried.

"*How*? How do you not understand? We aren't meant to be here; in this time, in this place, with these people. They aren't like us, don't you see that? Why doesn't anyone see that? You all look at me like I'm crazy; like *I've* lost my mind. But I'm not the one who's lost it! Do you have any idea what it feels like getting on a plane after saying goodbye to your family, about to start this great adventure in college...to have it all ripped away?!"

"Ruby," I speak slowly after struggling to a sitting position.

"We *all* know what it feels like. We didn't choose to be taken from everything and everyone we know. And we don't think you're crazy. We know you're just upset-"

"*Upset*?! Oh really? I'm just *upset*? Oh! Poor little Ruby! She's just a kid! She doesn't understand anything because she's not old enough to. Let's coddle her instead of listening to her because she doesn't know what she's talking about! She's too young! Walking around in the world without being able to fully understand anything!"

I wince. "That's not what I meant and you know it! Yes, you are young and yes, you are upset. But we aren't coddling you! You just need to cool down and realize we *aren't abandoning you*. Why do you keep trying to make us?"

"Trying to make you?! You know what? I'm done! Look at you all high and mighty! Sitting there, even now when you can't move, acting like you're so much better than me! You're not my mom! You're not my sister! You go on and on about how I'm so young and impressionable when you're TWENTY-ONE. Who do you think you are staring down at me like you're so much older and wiser! I'm *eighteen*, not some kid. I'm not stupid or too young to understand what I'm seeing!"

I sat there with wide eyes, stunned. My mouth opened but I was not really sure how to respond. Was she right? I feel so much older than her but I'm really not. It was probably for the best that I couldn't respond because she was not done.

She stood up, walking away from me, and began to pace. As she yelled, the rays of light extending in the dark from the lantern lit up the area between us. It brightened the dark enough I could see spittle shooting from her mouth with certain words.

"You want to know why I did what I did? Fine! I'll tell you! I really thought you people were just blind to the truth staring back at you. But I guess you all just don't care if we never make it back home. I bet you don't have a family back there! That would make sense for you! Or maybe it's just *so great* being popular now that who cares if it's even possible."

I frowned as anger sparked inside me. My eyes narrowed and I shook a little at her having the audacity to think she was the only one whose life had come crashing down around her.

"My life is gone! And you all prance around like it's over while I sit at night staring at the stars and wondering if my family misses me; what they're doing; if I'll be alone for the rest of my life! I thought if I could get you away and remind you how awful this place is that you would finally understand. But I was wrong." Ruby's voice broke off at the end and she turned away from me, but not before I saw the tears shining in her eyes.

I sighed, feeling my anger drain a little to once more be replaced with pity. Rubbing my temple, I felt a headache coming on. This, in turn, made me feel ashamed.

Part of me still thought she needed to realize she was wrong. But then part of me was questioning if what she said didn't have some truth to it. *Did* I ignore thoughts of the world I grew up in for the world I was now in? I did have parents but we weren't close. I was sure they loved me in their own way but I doubted they were too upset when they learned I was missing. I had no close friends in high school or college. I had no past boyfriends. I was missing nothing by being here. I was really gaining every-thing by being *here*. But was I allowing that to cloud my judg-ment with everything? Was I ignoring other people and a possibility for them to get back to their families? Was I supposed to stay here?

No, no. I shook my head to clear those thoughts. They weren't any I hadn't had before and I knew I still agreed with what I came to terms with the many other times I had asked myself those questions. Who knew what life would have been like before. Yes, families would have more time together. But there was *no* plausible way for us to get back. Besides, wasn't it better for us to remember those we loved as they were and not as they would be when everything started to go bad, with no future in sight?

Looking up at Ruby my eyes softened some more. Still, I felt like she needed guidance. Not really because of her age, as I may have unknowingly suggested, but because of how she acted.

"Listen Ruby. I'm sorry. You're right that we kind of walk on eggshells around you. Everyone has the same thoughts you have. Everyone misses their family and their pets and their lives. But, nothing we can do is going to fix that. We need to come to terms that *this* is our life now. That is the only way we have a chance at being happy and at having a future here."

She whipped around so fast her blonde braid swung and hit her cheek. "I don't want a future here! I don't want to settle!"

"I know. I know. But we don't have a say in it. In none of this. The sooner you understand that the sooner everything can be better. I know it's sad, the thought of all that you've lost, and I know you don't believe me when I say you aren't alone. But you're not alone, Ruby. I won't leave you. I forgive you for what happened tonight and everyone else will too. Just come back with me to the pack. Please."

"That's just it! I don't want your forgiveness. I don't want to go back where I'm reminded nonstop that nothing is the same and everyone has already moved on!

I frowned in fear as a shiver of foreboding went through my body. "Ruby, what do you mean?"

She turned towards me from her place near the trees I had stumbled through earlier. "Despite what you may think of me, I know we can't go back. But that doesn't mean I'm fine living this life I've been forced into. I had hoped you'd come with me. But I know you won't, now. I'm leaving."

"What? No! You don't know what you're saying! Please just come back with me! We can talk about this. You don't know what it's like out there! Danger is everywhere. There are no hotels or restaurants! You won't survive, Ruby!"

She shook her head. "My mind's made up. If this is what my life's going to be like now, I'm not spending it here like a bird in a cage or someone who is seen as a little girl or a baby machine. I'm leaving."

She began to walk away as I pleaded for her to stay. Right before the darkness completely swallowed her up, she stopped and met my eyes.

"I really am sorry, you know. Not for what I believe or why I did it. But I *do* regret how I went about it. I never meant to hurt anyone. Or make anyone do anything they didn't want to do. That's the reason why I have to leave, after all." She hesitated and then a small smile graced her lips. "You know, despite what I said...you kind of are like the closest thing I have to a sister now. Thank you for everything you did and tried to do for me. Maybe one day we'll see each other again but I can't be this person anymore. I can't stay here any longer and watch you all just accept what's being thrown at you. Goodbye, Ava."

I struggled from my place on the forest floor, trying to get up and go to her, before collapsing. "Please Ruby. Don't go! No one's trying to alienate you or make you do something you don't want to do. Ruby! Stop!"

Then she was gone.

I looked down at the lantern she left next to me and hit the ground in frustration. I could barely move and I sat there unable to do anything to stop her while she left. Before I could do anything or think of anything else, a twig snapped behind me.

I turned around as fast as I could, internally groaning at the sore feeling radiating down my body from the movement. I didn't see anything at first. Then I saw a glint. Squinting in its direction I saw the glint become golden eyes. It was a shifter.

It had been a long time since I had seen Leo's wolf form. I could vaguely recall what it looked like and I could barely see it in the dark now. But I knew the sense of rightness that filled me. A feeling of safety filled me. It could only mean one thing. Leo had finally found me.

I cried out in relief. Ignoring the pain, I slowly turned my body to try and face the direction he was coming from.

"Leo!"

The wolf emerged from the woods before it shifted to that of a naked Leo. One I shouldn't have had trouble looking away from, given how much pain I was in, but a girl could only be so strong.

Blushing, I quickly looked up to his eyes as he pulled me into his arms and practically onto his lap.

"Ava, Mine. I was so worried." He kissed my forehead, cheeks, and then mouth. Pulling away he growled as his eyes ran over my body. "Look at you! Who did this to you?"

I winced but gave a sheepish smile. "Ironically, the trees and myself. For just about all of it."

"Just about? Who hurt you?! Where?" He snarled even as his hands and eyes searched my body. I could just tell he was cataloging everything.

"I'm fine."

"No, you're not fine! You're crying!" Even in his human form, his eyes were still glowing and I could tell he was ticked off.

"Because I'm happy to see you?" I said almost like I was asking a question. I was hoping to have him relax a little. As much as I didn't want Ruby gone, him snapping on her since she was probably still close by would not help anyone.

He growled and gripped my face, forcing me to meet his eyes. "You were crying before I snapped that twig. Please. Tell me where it hurts the most and who hurt you, Mine."

I could practically feel my heart melt at his concern and awareness. "You snapped the twig on purpose?"

"Of course. I didn't want to scare you. Now stop avoiding my questions!" He huffed.

I smiled and just had to peck him on the lips again, quickly. Pulling back I reluctantly answered. "Honestly, I didn't realize I was crying. I do hurt... everywhere. But I think it's a bit of that and... Ruby."

Almost like my emotions were agreeing with my assumption, fresh tears came to my eyes. Leo visibly softened and wrapped his arms around me.

"I heard. I've been looking for you for what seems like way

too long now. After finding out who convinced the townspeople to attack and Ruby's involvement and you being missing... I wasn't in the best headspace. I'm not going to lie, I was the closest I've ever been to attacking a woman when I heard the two of you yelling and came."

I pulled back with wide eyes. Just enough to read his face. "Really? What stopped you?"

He gave me a wry yet soft smile. "You. As soon as I saw you, I calmed down enough to realize you were trying to get her to come back. I figured she wasn't a threat to you...anymore." He shook his head in confusion. "I guess I was also a bit confused. When I left to find you, Ruby was with everyone else. A bunch of people went to confront her and did. Alpha Gabriel and this human named O'Connor. Then they left to find me and tell me what they learned. Ruby was supposed to be under guard. I spent forever trying to find you, Mine. And the human girl who was being watched managed to sneak away from a bunch of shifters and find you in the middle of a dark forest first."

He shook his head, the wrinkle of his nose and furrowed brows leading me to think he really was confused by his statement.

"How? Why was it so hard for you to find me?" My voice broke a little and he wrapped me back in his arms, comforting me. "I've been waiting for someone to come. I tried so hard to get back on my own, and I really did make it far. I think. But I only made it so far before I knew I needed help or serious rest before I could have enough energy to get back. I don't know if I'm just that out of shape or if it's all of this pain my body is in. Maybe it's both. But the first time someone did find me, it was Ruby."

"Normally I would be able to scent you and find you fast. But with the fire... all that I can smell is smoke. Of course, when we're finally mated we will have a bond I could trace. Something that will always connect us. But right now?" He took a shaky breath. "I'm just glad I've finally found you."

I blushed softly at the thought of us finally mating. But I

pushed it aside. "So, you heard all of what Ruby said? That she decided to leave?"

He nodded and looked at me sadly. "Yes. I'm sorry, Mine. I know how much she means to you."

I sniffed as the thought came to mind. "It's all my fault! I should've done something to make her stay!" Maybe if I had just spent more time with her. Or if I had just listened to her when it first became obvious how upset she was.

He growled. "No, it's not. You tried your best. Before and tonight. I heard. Yes, she's young but she is an adult. Her decisions are her own, and I hate to say it, baby. But you trying to force her to stay would've just made her think she was right for the way she thinks staying here is like."

I brushed my hands against my cheeks, wiping my tears. "You're right. It just hurts. I feel like I could've done more. If not tonight then before."

"My beautiful mate. My strong and caring Luna. You can only help those who want to be helped." He kissed me, his lips parting mine to deepen the kiss for a quick second before pulling away. "But enough of that." He gave me a stern look. "It didn't escape my notice, you've still managed to not answer my questions. I know of Ruby's involvement. But I want to know what happened tonight and who hurt you."

I winced but nodded. "Fine, I'll tell you. But first, can we go back? I really do hurt and I feel so disgusting."

Alarmed, Leo pulls back to stare at my body. "Oh no! I'm so dumb! Of course, baby. We'll get you back to the packhouse! I'll have a bath made for you even if I have to get the water from the stream. It'll help your sore muscles as you clean yourself off."

"You're my hero. You know that, right?" I smiled up at him lovingly.

He grinned. "Of course I am. It's my job to care for you; to love and protect you. Whether it's your physical health, your mental health, from a situation, or from yourself. I'll always protect you. Be that as it may, I think in this specific situation you were your own hero. You got yourself this far. Just needed a little help to make it the rest of the way."

I smiled at him happily. My stomach felt fluttery, like when I used to write in my novels that someone had butterflies. This was exactly what that sounded like.

He lifted me from the ground and into his arms, after handing me the lantern. He grinned down at me and quipped, "We don't need to start another fire tonight."

I giggled and agreed, then wrapped one arm around his neck to hold on. The other arms dutifully holding the lantern.

"Once we're done getting you all cleaned up, I'll feed you and you'll tell me all about what happened."

"You just had to get that in again, didn't you?" I laughed.

He looked almost affronted. "Of course. You're the most important thing in my life. You *are* my life. I almost lost you tonight and I need to know everything so it won't happen again."

I smiled softly as I stared up into his face. "It's okay. Your protectiveness is one of the many reasons why I love you."

Just as we *finally* broke through the tree line into the pack's clearing, he stopped suddenly. He stared down at me with wide eyes, an almost amazed look in them, and a slowly growing smile.

Well, I did say I was going to tell him I loved him as soon as possible. I grinned up at him happily just as people began to rush over.

CHAPTER TWENTY-TWO

L eo and I didn't get to talk about my revelation after that. At least, not immediately.

The next few hours were emotionally and physically draining; spent answering question after question then helping injured people. Leo had tried to push it off a few hours, insisting I was tired, injured, and needing to rest.

After Gabriel insisted on me debriefing them, reminding us how important it was to know who, why, and what to protect the territory, I agreed. Convincing Leo was a bit harder until I suggested we could eat while there. That way when we were done we could go straight upstairs and not have to come back down for food.

When I agreed, though, I did not expect it to take so long. Maybe they could feel I wasn't giving them the whole story. But, despite everything that happened, I didn't necessarily want the women caught. I didn't think they'd hurt them. But, the shifter had chosen to give herself a mission in life. Even if I didn't agree with how she was doing it, I did recognize how important it was. I didn't want her to be stopped. At least, not because of me.

With Ruby, well after how we parted I knew forcing her back

here would just make things worse. For everyone. Don't get me wrong, I wanted her to come back. Hopefully, though, wherever she was she was safe and would come to realize she had been wrong. The packs weren't trying to force people to stay or do anything against their will. When we first came, they were our saviors; rescuing us from the plane crash and potentially worst situations. Those of us who left *should* have realized how lucky we were.

The world we now lived in was one none of us knew how to navigate. Yet, Ruby had lucked out with not having to really experience any of the outside dangers. She didn't understand how we needed a place to keep us safe and teach us how to live in the world before we were thrust into it. Between those reasons and the reality that they could possibly never have wives or mates if they didn't meet with us; well it wasn't a super big deal when they asked us to stay until they saw if there were other mates amongst our numbers. They *did* promise no one would be forced to do anything, even if they were a mate. I mean, while we were waiting to meet all these new shifters we were given places to stay, food, and now training on things like growing crops or self-defense. I genuinely could not see why Ruby had such an issue with it. But that didn't mean I wanted to be the reason why she was forced back here. Convincing her to come back, if we could find her, would be one thing. But after all that happened recently, I doubted she could be convinced any time soon.

So, yes, I exempted some things when I was telling them what had happened. I told them what Ruby had done and how I came to be knocked out, and subsequently kidnapped. Even if I didn't consider what had happened was a kidnapping. I mean, I woke up in the same woods I had been knocked out in and let go soon after.

I told them vague information about how the woman was indeed the person traveling around the place, rescuing women from men who bought them from The Gathering. "In fact, that's how Ruby got her to try and take me. Even if I was a shifter's mate, she's made it her goal to rescue those who were taken against their will. Ruby just didn't tell her I didn't need or want rescuing."

We once more sat in Gabriel's office for the conversation. Leo kept me on his lap, refusing to let me go. While I felt both like rolling my eyes and smiling happily at the fact, it was useful to calm him each time he growled in anger at parts of my story. He was so loving that between holding me to him and his growls reverberating up my body, he would raise a sandwich to my lips each time I wasn't talking.

Gabriel did try to get more out of me. I wasn't *really* withholding information. I was just choosing my words carefully. Like, I wasn't coming straight out and saying the woman was a shifter. But I was addressing her mannerisms when I woke up and what she said. I also didn't tell them about how I thought this mission was a personal one. It was not necessary to tell them what happened.

"See, I don't think we have anything to worry about from her. Anymore." I corrected myself when the rumblings filled the room. "This was all because of Ruby...and even she regretted how things went down. She told me when she left."

"The thing is, Luna, we have no guarantee this won't happen again. What if Ruby can't let go of her anger towards us and starts something again? Or this woman...what happens when a shifter next finds his mate at The Gathering and *has* to buy her to avoid all-out war? Will she try and take more mates?"

I sighed at Gabriel's understandable statement, even if it wasn't what I wanted them to start thinking about. I quickly chewed and swallowed the bite of food in my mouth, at Leo's insistence, before objecting.

"I really don't think that will happen. I mean, she let me go when I told her I wasn't being held against my will. Besides, I understand what she's trying to do. She's not trying to hurt people or take people away from loving relationships. Only those who are in need of help."

"And we understand that. We personally can agree with that. But as leaders who have to keep some semblance of control and agreement with the humans, we can't keep Gatherers out of the surrounding area by our clear abhorrence of kidnapping, then not do anything when someone else is kidnapping women."

My mouth opened in objection. It was not the same thing.

Gabriel shook his head and finished speaking, stopping any objection I had. "Even if we agree with what she's doing. It's politics. A thin line is what we walk to keep the peace between shifters and humans. No exceptions can be made."

My breath came out in a huff of annoyance, but I understood what he was saying. "She's not the one who did all this, though. Ruby started all of this. And that was all my fault-"

Leo's snarl cut through my sentence. "No. It. Wasn't. This happened at no fault of yours, Mine. I told you that before. She may have not had ill intentions for you all, but she chose her path."

"But I was her friend! I was supposed to be there for her after I realized she wasn't happy here. Before that, even. If I had just paid attention to her more, I could have stopped all of this."

The man who responded to me was one of the plane crash survivors. I had seen him before at times, but I had never talked to him before. He must be that O'Connor person Leo had mentioned before. The one who helped them when I was gone.

He was attractive in a dark and dangerous kind of way. He screamed deadly. His eyes were dark, sharp, and calculating. Things I could see associated with a soldier based on books I had read.

"You and I both know that would have done nothing. She's 18, an adult in age. But her mentality is one of a rebellious teen who wants things her way. One who thinks she's an adult and thinks she knows everything but sees things in shades of only black and white. She doesn't understand all that goes on. Only sees what she wants to. Nothing you or anyone could have said or done would have helped this. This is something that teens have done since...forever. The only way this gets fixed is for her to grow up, mentally. And the only way that'll happen is for it to be forced upon her or her to change herself."

I winced a little. He was right. Now that he had said it, I could see the similarities between her and just about every rebellious teen I had ever read about, watched on TV, or encountered in life.

My voice came out small. "That doesn't mean we should just let her be forced into situations that will make her grow up. And that's what will happen if she's out there on her own."

Leo agreed. "We'll try and track her down. Bring her back."

I started shaking my head before he was done. "No, no. That would just make things worse. He's right..." I nodded my head towards O'Connor. "If she doesn't decide to come back on her own, it'll just make things worse."

O'Connor nodded. "I'll track her down. I can try and keep her safe if or until she decides to come back."

"Really? You'd do that? How are you going to track her down?"

There was a glint in his eyes I couldn't tell the meaning of. "She's just a kid *and* she's one of us. Of course, I'd do that. Besides, tracking's kind of my thing."

After more talking, more questions, and more being fed by Leo we were done. The relief and exhaustion which hit me were almost instantaneous. I couldn't wait to get back to our room to take a bath, clean my many wounds, and sleep. Not necessarily in that order.

Leo lifted me in his arms and we left to stop just as fast. There were quite a few people who were still injured and needing help. Most looked like humans who were ones from the town.

Even though I barely had any energy and was injured myself, I made Leo put me in a chair. Whether they were our attackers or not, they had injuries worse than mine. I couldn't in good conscience go upstairs to relax and sleep while they were still hurting.

Leo wasn't happy with it. Not because he didn't care about them but because he cared about me more. In the end, he hovered around me while I sat and helped others, waiting for the moment I was done to whisk me away hours later.

The next morning came with me groaning and blinking groggily at the bright light streaming through the window. Everything hurt; my body, my head, even my eyes. A thick arm pulled me closer to a warm body, bringing a gentle smile to my face.

Not wanting to attempt moving just yet I ran my fingers along his arm, tracing veins and light brown arm hair. Even in his sleep, he was happy with me touching him because there were soft, yet deep noises coming from him. If I didn't know any better I would think it was a purr. A grin tugged at the corners of my lips at the thought. If he had heard that I just know he would have something to say about it.

My exploration of his arm must have woke him up because the next thing I knew his nose was nuzzling into my neck. I giggled and flinched away.

"Stop, that tickles."

His breath blew across the side of my neck as he chuckled and continued to nuzzle me. When he spoke my entire body vibrated from his chest. "Come now, Mine. You know you like it."

I laughed and jerked away, groaning from the soreness in my body and laughing from the ticklish feeling he kept giving me both at the same time. My neck was one of the biggest ticklish spots of my body.

"No! No, please. Stop!" I kept squirming and laughing.

He chuckled and finally stopped, kissing me on the neck he

had just been tickling and then pulling me back to his body. This time, though, I was on my back and able to see him.

"You know you love that, baby. Love me." He said it teasingly but there was a soft look in his eyes.

My smile softened as I looked up at him. Raising my hand to his face I nodded. "Yes, I do. I love you."

The happiness that spread across his face was breathtaking. He leaned down to kiss my lips once, and then twice. Pulling back he smiled down at me. "I love you too."

I grinned cheekily, "I know."

He laughed, throwing his head back. "Of course you do! I've never made it a secret. But I won't ever stop letting you know."

I laughed softly with him and then shook my head. "I know. But you show me and tell me every day, in everything you do. I don't know how I got so lucky. And I don't know why I fought it so long. I'm sorry for that. I feel like I wasted so much time."

The furrow between his brow wiped away his smile as he shook his head. Then he grabbed my face to make sure I met his eyes. "Listen to me, Ava. *I'm* the lucky one here. And if you insist on it, I could be persuaded to say we are both lucky. But it won't really make a difference. You gave me a chance to live. A chance I never would have gotten before."

His face softened and he leaned down to give me an Eskimo kiss, brushing his nose against mine. Then he continued. "And there's nothing you need to be sorry for, Mine. You needed time to adjust to...everything. I always knew that. I understand that. Don't ever feel sorry about anything, my Luna. Let alone that."

"Yes, but after everything that happened yesterday...being attacked and not knowing if I'd ever see you again, even for a brief moment, was horrible. I didn't want to have wasted our time or never be able to tell you how I felt. I don't want to go through life not knowing what it's like to truly be with the love of my life."

He pulled away to look at me, a serious look on his face. His eyes kept moving fast between mine, looking for something. "Do y- are you saying what I think you're saying?"

I nodded, my eyes cutting to the side and then back shyly. Licking my lips, I prayed for some more courage. After taking a deep breath I nodded again, looking up at him with a pink tint to my cheeks. "Yes, I am."

"But...I thought you wanted to wait longer. Until we know each other better; until we go home."

I shook my head. I had given a lot of thought to this, going back and forth. Making sure I wasn't just making a decision based on fear. But I knew it wasn't like that. I had been waiting for someone like him my entire life and didn't realize it. I wasn't going to wait any longer.

"I don't want to wait any longer. We've waited long enough and yesterday just helped me realize. I don't want to spend another moment not being your mate. In more than just name, that is."

At his silence I began to get nervous, trying to read his face. Did I make a mistake? Did he want to wait? But he ended my panic quickly, as he smiled and brushed my hair back.

"You're sure? Really sure?"

I nodded. "I am...are you? I can wait-"

His kiss cut me off. Pulling back after a few moments he gave a mischievous look. "I hope you're not hungry. I may act like a gentleman but I've been holding back. It hasn't been easy wait-ing. Now that I have you we aren't leaving this room until you're completely mine."

I blushed but nodded. Leaning up, I kissed his lips then kept kissing up the length of his jawline to his ears. Then I whispered, "Then make me yours quickly, Mate. You know how much I enjoy my food."

He growled playfully and lunged at me, rolling on top of my body and nibbling my lips. "Don't worry...you won't be thinking of food for a while, Mine."

I laughed and as we kissed I knew he was right. I didn't care about anything but beginning our future...finally.

The next time I woke up it was because of my stomach growling. I looked over, feeling my cheeks heat, as Leo chuckled. My head was resting on his arm but he was laying on his side staring down at me.

As my cheeks felt even hotter I just knew I was blushing brightly. "Are you watching me? How long have you been awake?"

"A while. I wanted to watch my sleeping mate. You're almost even more beautiful in your sleep." He shook his head ruefully. "I don't even know how that's possible."

I bit my lip and looked away shyly. "Why didn't you wake me? What time is it even?"

"You needed your sleep. You were out around three hours, now. I guess I wore you out."

I gasped and shoved his chest playfully. "You did not!"

His laugh barreled through him so much my whole body was jostled. "Okay, okay. We wore each other out?"

I shook my head and huffed with a grin. "Keep it up, mister and it'll be a while before that happens again!"

Still laughing he raised his free hand in surrender. "Okay! I'll stop. Promise." His entire face was still alight with his humor.

I smiled up at him and leaned up to kiss him just as my stomach growled again. Groaning, I covered my face in embarrassment.

At his laugh, my fingers spread enough to see him. When I saw his smug smile my hand fell. "What exactly is that look for?"

"I told you I'd have you forgetting all about food."

I gasped and shoved him again, trying to hide my smile. "Leo!"

He chuckled, kissed my nose, and then nuzzled my neck.

After a few moments of him inhaling my scent, now entwined with his according to him, he leaned back to kiss me once more. "Let's go get you fed, my mate."

When I went to roll out of bed with him I groaned. Between everything that happened yesterday and then this morning my body was super sore. I was not looking forward to how sore I'd be tomorrow. They said the 2nd day was the worst.

At my groan, Leo stopped and rushed to my side. "What? What's wrong?"

I smiled gently, though it felt more like a grimace. "I'm alright. Just sore." My eyes widened at the look on his face. "From yesterday."

He growled softly. "I knew I shouldn't have let us mate when you were still hurt."

"Stop. Don't do that. I wasn't that hurt and I don't regret anything we did. Just...didn't think about how sore my entire body would be today."

Leaning down to peck me on my lips he grinned wolfishly. That was the only way I could think to describe it. "Don't worry, Mine. I'll carry you anywhere you need to be for as long as you need."

I felt like there was a permanent blush on my face today. "Fine. Let's get dressed and get food...unless you wanna go grab some food for us and bring it back." The latter came out in a hopeful question.

A pout fell on his lips and it was both adorable and amusing. "I wanted to show you off, though."

I groaned. "Please. For me? It's already going to be super embarrassing whenever we do end up going down, knowing they'll all know what we've done."

"Baby, it really won't be that bad. They'll all be happy for us and envious. They would never make you feel embarrassed. Anyway, I already figured you'd want to stay here longer. I linked with one of our packmates still here to have some warm water brought up before you woke up. I'll grab it for you and fill the tub. Then, while you soak in your well-deserved bath I'll go get us food."

I smiled up at him lovingly. "I love you so much, Leo. Thank you."

He grinned down at me happily. "Anything for my Luna." He pecked me on the lips one more time then stood to go grab the water jugs from the hallway. Before opening the door he stopped and looked back at me softly. "I will always love you. There is no time limit. Nothing will ever stop it. Until the end of time and beyond that."

We ended up staying in our room until the next day; two days after the attack on the pack and Ruby's departure.

Part of me felt I should feel guilty about disappearing when there was so much to be done, but I couldn't find it in me to feel anything but happiness. Well, happiness and the ache radiating throughout my body, which was worse today. Leo had wanted me to stay in bed longer since the worst of it was my feet and legs. We were pretty sure I had sprained an ankle. But, though I wasn't feeling guilty over spending the day before in our room, I knew another day spent hiding out would have rubbed me the wrong way.

Going downstairs for breakfast, I wasn't sure what to expect. But it wasn't what I found.

No one was in the halls or rooms we passed. There was complete silence except for a slight humming coming from the kitchen.

When we walked in I stopped in amused shock. Silver was the only one in the kitchen, dancing and humming as he cooked what looked like a feast.

Before I could say anything he turned around with a smirk on his lips. "Welcome lovebirds! I'm currently working on your..." His head tilted as he thought then grinned at me. "On your mate day feast."

The glimmer in his eyes made me feel like that had not been what he planned on saying. But the heat spreading up my neck and to my cheeks made me want to turn back around to avoid responding.

However, Silver and I had a unique relationship. One that meant I had to respond, but I could respond just as playfully as he. After all, we were friends. Not that I had ever had a friendship like this one before.

I narrowed my eyes playfully and said. "It better be tacos and enchiladas and whatever else I can dream of if you don't expect to be smacked for that."

Silver and Leo laughed at that, Silver raising his hands in surrender while Leo bent to kiss my cheek.

"It is, don't worry! It's why I'm all by myself in here."

"Speaking of which... Where is everyone?" I looked around the kitchen, inhaling the delicious scents of food and spices filling the kitchen.

"Outside. Another reason why I'm in here cooking....and cooking a lot. Alpha Gabriel's gotten them all to start cleaning up, cutting down the trees too burnt to save...everyone's out there helping. Even the humans from town. At least, the ones from yesterday."

My brow raised and I exchanged a look with Leo. "Really? They're still here?"

Silver nodded as he turned back towards the food. Continuing to cook as he talked. "Yea. He didn't want them gone until they helped fix as much as possible. Both as a way to have help and to make sure they had no more doubts about people being here on their own terms." He tossed a look back at Leo. "You can get food for you two, by the way. Don't mind me."

Leo snarled, baring his teeth. But his grin made it clear he was just playing. "I don't need permission to take care of my mate, thanks very much."

I smacked Leo's arm playfully but laughed as Silver turned to roll his eyes playfully at me.

As Leo joined Silver moving around the kitchen to make us

breakfast, I settled on a barstool. I had given up on making our food if Leo was in the room.

"So, how's everything outside? Is it really bad?"

Silver shook his head. "No, not really in my opinion. Really just the land and the trees."

"And he's wanting it to be cleaned and forgotten?"

"Exactly. If anything, the major damage is in the relationship with the town and the feeling of security."

Leo came over with our food and sat down. He didn't stop there. Instead, he reached over, grabbed my toast, and raised it to my mouth. I huffed in amused exasperation, my brow raising at him even as I leaned forward to take a bite.

"I told you I could feed myself."

He chuckled and leaned forward to kiss my nose. "And I told you... I have many, many jobs when it comes to you. Making sure you're fed is one of them. Just so happens I enjoy taking to that task with a hands-on approach."

I laughed and shook my head. When I glanced over towards Silver I saw him turning away with an unreadable look in his eye. Was he envious? I could see why but it would make things harder around here if we caused him to be upset every time we were near each other.

Turning back to Leo I saw him give me a small, sad smile and barely perceptible nod. So I had seen right and he had noticed too.

Hoping to fill the silence, I started to continue eating. "So...what does Gabriel plan on doing with the town humans after? I mean the fact they've seen the territory. Didn't he say he tried to keep the townspeople away?"

Both of them nodded but it was Leo who answered this time. "I think he's hoping the longer he keeps them here the more they'll...I don't know, be more inclined to keep it a secret."

I nodded slowly, thinking about it. I guess it made sense in a way. Make it where they had no doubts or issues, so they are fine keeping things like the territory layout secret as opposed to feeling forced to keep a secret.

After we finished eating and Leo washed the dishes, mainly because it still hurt to walk on my feet from being attacked by so many branches and tree roots, I offered to help Silver in the kitchen while Leo went outside to help.

It took many minutes to reassure Leo that Silver was just my friend and I would only help with stuff from my seat. Even then I had to remind Leo that I was now wearing his mark and completely mated to him, so he had nothing to worry about. Besides, after a brief scare the day before, we now both knew how to use our mate link and were able to speak in each other's minds. I was still getting used to that but he seemed ecstatic at the idea.

After a few hours the food and I, much to my dismay, were carried outside for what I liked to call linner. It was past lunchtime but much too early to truly be considered dinner, even if it was probably going to be the last meal of the day.

Silver had truly outdone himself and had somehow managed to cook enough food to feed an army in a few hours, all by himself. There were things to make tacos, enchilada platters, tamales, and more. Though, as Silver explained to me while I helped him, these people wouldn't really be getting an authentic Mexican cuisine experience since he had to work with ingredients available here.

The meal was to both celebrate our mating and try and bring some semblance of security back to everyone here. Maybe even to highlight the similarities of how normal shifters were to the townspeople there. I had hoped Silver had just been joking about the mating part of the equation, but apparently not.

It was set up like a dinner buffet and we all sat on the ground or tree logs. I looked around. The damage from the fires didn't look too bad just as Silver had said. Mostly, it seemed to be giving the pack more lumber and clearing space. If you ignored the charred grass and the burned trees that were still standing.

Looking at that, I could understand what Silver had meant by the damage being more to the feeling of security for people here. With the constant reminder of how much worse it could have been, I could see why people would be unsettled. I mean, heck, I was the only one kidnapped and I wasn't as upset as many of the other people looked.

I spent the entire meal stuffing myself to my delight while being completely embarrassed by all the well-wishers coming up to Leo and me. Needless to say, at the end of the day I was mentally exhausted even when I did nowhere near the amount of work everyone else had.

The meal ran long after the sunset and the lanterns came out. When people finally began to stop eating it seemed to turn into a party. There was singing and dancing; laughter and fun.

I leaned into Leo from my seat on his lap. He was sitting on the ground with his back against the building wall and hadn't wanted me to sit on the floor. Yawning, I nuzzled my face into the crook of his neck.

"Tired, Mine?"

I nodded as I felt my eyes begin to droop. "I don't know why. I haven't done much yesterday or today."

He chuckled in a completely smug way if I had to describe it. "Well, I did keep you up most of the night after keeping my out busy yesterday. And that was after seeing if your body could move through trees, and failing."

I gasped and pulled back. But I couldn't stop the smile from crossing my lips. "How mean."

He laughed aloud then leaned forward. Nuzzling my nose and then kissing my lips he whispered, "Sorry. But it's true."

He grinned as he leaned back when I tried to push him playfully. When I yawned again Leo bent his knees, slid his arms under me, and somehow rolled up to stand in a smooth transition I would never be able to do.

"Let's get you to bed, my mate. I promise to keep my hands to myself tonight and let you get some sleep."

As he carried me inside and up the stairs, I waited until I was sure no wolf ears would hear. Leaning back I grinned up at him cheekily. "And why would you do something like that?"

He growled down at me as his eyes darkened and then began to glow gold. With that, he began to bound up the stairs. Leading me to what I was pretty sure was guaranteed to be another sleepless night. But I wasn't complaining.

CHAPTER TWENTY-THREE

Two weeks later we had packed the few items we had, which mainly consisted of what Ana had given me. I had tried to give them back to her but she insisted, saying I was starting with nothing and she had enough to hold her over for now.

The way she had worded it had been weird to me, and when I tried to object again she finally told me that she was pregnant. She pointed out it would be a while she would be able to wear normal clothes again, and by then she could have more made. I guess it wasn't a secret because, apparently, after a point shifters can scent the differences when you are not pregnant versus when you are. I was not sure how I felt about that but I was glad she had at least told me. It at least explained the jovial atmosphere Gabriel and Ana's pack had lately. This was the first child they would have in I don't know how long, and it was their alpha's child at that.

We had all spent the past weeks continuing to clean, help build, and welcoming new packs. My favorite pack to come since Silver's was the first European pack that made it. Don't hold it against me but I am a sucker for accents. Especially European accents.

During these past weeks, I had continued helping Gabriel with writing about the packs that came, and the only European pack to have arrived so far was fascinating. European packs already had something the packs we had seen so far did not, a European Council. They had been hosting meetings every six months with all of the European pack leaders for, well, centuries.

I had laughed when I heard about that but no one else understood why. I had tried explaining to them it seemed like Europe had not changed because when I came from they had the European Union, but they all just kind of stared at me blankly.

The European Council also had been having pack get-togethers annually for mateless shifters. It rotated locations each year so shifters would also be able to explore different human-populated towns. It was an impressive system, to say the least, and had resulted in a couple of mates being found each year. It did not seem like much considering that only a few mates were found out of every European pack, but it was when I consider how often the American packs have found mates.

After the pack came they told us how long we would have to wait for the rest of the packs to get here.

After hearing that last week, Silver finally decided he needed to leave. He told us he had stayed longer than he should have, especially with the attack and everything. His pack needed him and they were coming up on another move soon. Since every-thing was getting back to normal around Gabriel's pack, and no other pack would be here soon, Silver thought it was the perfect time to leave.

I was upset at the fact I would maybe not see him again but he promised he would keep in touch. He had left the next day after giving me a few of my favorite recipes and telling me how to make the main ingredients. He had even offered a few alterna-tive ingredients that he could think of off the top of his head, seeing how I would not be near Mexico when Leo and I went back. Which was happening sooner than I had planned.

Leo and I had our first small argument yesterday after he was contacted by his pack. *Our pack. Remember that.* As I sat in our room for the last time here, I thought back to yesterday with a cringe.

"Hey, Mine. We need to talk."

I smiled as I turned to him from the kitchen stool I sat on. Papers were spread all across the kitchen bar as I had been finishing the pack ledger I was working on.

I had been working on putting all of the necessary information for each pack in a book for Gabriel before I decided to copy it for the other Alphas. I had done one for Gabriel, Leo, Silver, and the one European Alpha so far.

When I turned to Leo my smile had fallen at the serious look on his face. "What's wrong?"

"Apparently, we are needed back home. Beta Marcus linked me. He didn't tell me what it was but...it's serious. We need to go back tomorrow."

"What?! Tomorrow? Woah, woah, woah. Wait a second. We can't leave."

"I'm sorry, baby but we have to. If Beta Marcus says it's serious, it's serious."

Though I had not been around Marcus long, and for what felt like a very long time, I vividly remembered how laidback he was. Until he needed to be serious, of course. So, I understood what Leo was saying. If Marcus said it was serious then it was. But that didn't mean I could just drop everything here and leave.

"I can't just go! What about all of the people here? My people? They are still here waiting for all of these packs to arrive and I could never see them again! I can't leave yet."

"Yes, but our pack is your people now too and they need us now. These humans here will be fine without us. They're safe and settled. And I'm sorry, Mine. I really am. I don't like the thought you may not see them again if they happen to be mates.

But if they aren't mates I promise to bring you back to see them again. But we can't stay here."

"Well...what if you go and I stay. You can fix what's wrong and come back. I know they should be safe now and they're secure. But I'm one of the people they see as a liaison to Gabriel and the other shifters!"

His growl shocked me a little but I could tell it was him being irritated about the idea of me staying and not really at me.

"You're not staying here! You're my mate, my Luna. We aren't going to be separated. Never!"

He snarled, pacing back and forth in the kitchen. If he had been in his wolf form I was sure his hackles would be raised.

Seeing how upset he was, I slid off the stool and walked over to him. As soon as my arms had wrapped around him he immediately stopped, burying his nose in my neck. I stood there, not feeling ticklish for once because I knew him inhaling my scent was helping calm him down.

"I'm sorry," I whispered. "I didn't mean to upset you. I just...torn. Leaving here feels so...permanent. Like I'm losing the last bit of the life I knew. It's not that I don't want to go with you."

After a few moments, Leo pulled back to rest his forehead on mine. "I'm sorry too, Mine. I realize what you meant. The idea of being separated from you again is just...terrifying. But I know why you said it. But I promise you unless they're mates and leave before we get back...I'll bring you back to see them one day. They'll be fine here. They've been around Gabriel's pack...what...four months now? And since the attack, the doctor has really stepped up with being in communication with Gabriel. I know you may not want to hear it...but these people don't really need you anymore. You've helped them all you can now. But our pack needs us."

After we talked for a few more minutes, I asked when he thought we could maybe come back. His wince should have been my first clue. He told me about how long it would take us to travel to our pack and back, not including how long it would take to handle whatever issue that was happening.

I winced again, thinking back on that. We would not be coming back anytime soon. So, when we had talked to everyone about it last night, it became clear we were saying goodbye. Even if I was hoping to see them again.

Leo was right and my place was no longer here. It took me a while to come to terms with that. But, after experiencing being away from him before I knew I didn't want to do that again. I mean, we were not even mated before and it was something I never wanted to go through again. I could not imagine being away from him for months. Besides, he was right. When we had mated we started a new chapter of our lives. This was part of that.

Considering the fact we were leaving, and with our fight yesterday that still weighed on me even though it was minor, I had also decided to mention I thought the female shifter was in fact shifter.

I guess part of me hoped I would not have the secret on my conscience any longer. Especially seeing how I would not be at Gabriel's pack territory much longer. I figured she must have gotten far enough away they could not track her by now, and the packs would also be able to know there was an unknown female shifter out there.

Of course, the shocking turn of events did not stop with just us announcing we needed to leave.

After we told everyone we had to leave and would be leaving immediately, it was not such a big deal as I thought it would be. Then the two kids from the plane crash came out of the main house and shocked everyone. The teenage girl finally talked.

We still did not know her name and she did not say much, but what she did say then had caused an uproar. The protests continued when Liam, the boy ever-present by her side, agreed with her. What had been us saying goodbye to everyone had turned into debates and arguments.

Now it's way too early to be awake and my 'bags' are packed. I laugh to myself lightly at the generous idea of having bags packed.

I walk downstairs to see a couple of other bags on the floor by the door and I hear the many voices coming from the kitchen. When I walk in, I see everyone eating and talking. I smile and walk over to Leo, to be pulled onto his lap and fed.

After another hour we headed out to leave the packhouse and all of the survivors from the plane crash were waiting. Though they were saying goodbye to us, everyone's attention was on the two people standing next to me.

I looked over at Liam and the girl and asked softly, "Are you two sure you want to come with us?"

The girl only nodded while Liam grinned up at me, jumping from side to side in excitement.

I sighed but smiled softly. I did not know why the kids wanted to come with us. We had to make it clear to them this was not a quick vacation. If they wanted to come back it would not be anytime soon. But they were adamant. So much so that all protests yesterday had fallen on non-listening ears.

Leo wrapped his arm around my waist and bent to kiss me. After a few moments, he pulled away. "Ava Thorne...my mate."

I was startled a little at his last name after my name but then smiled as happiness trickled through me.

"Are you ready to go home, Mine?"

The six shifters from our pack who had stayed with us were getting the carriage ready. The same buggy that had brought me here. It had been so long since I was last in it and I was not the same person that had first arrived here. I had grown from a girl who preferred to hide in the corner of the room to someone who, well, still preferred to hide in my room. But, I had stood up for myself and I had become a leading figure. I had grown from scared, worried, and uncertain to someone who would try and stand up for what I believed in or wanted. I had made friends and lost friends. I had accepted my new life, building it into something I could be happy with. I had learned more about this new world I live in now than most people who grew up here knew. I had found love.

Smiling up at Leo happily, I nodded. Just yesterday I had wanted to stay here. But I realized that was fear and uncertainty speaking; that was the past me speaking. But I was finally ready to say hello to my future with this man by my side. I knew I could do anything with him helping me, supporting me, encouraging me, and loving me.

"Yes, Leo Thorne...my mate. Take me home."

SNEAK PEAK

~ The Female Shifter ~

The fire was bright against the night sky. The smoke wafted through the air, the crackle and pops from the fire, and the light itself drawing predators of every kind to her.

I shook my head from my crouched position on the tree branch, 20 feet in the air and five feet away from the aforementioned beacon of death.

It was ironic, truly. The fire was such a necessary part of living. Not just surviving, but also living. Especially for humans. A necessary source of heat for body warmth and cooking. A light in the darkness. The easiest way for water sterilization. But also, a method of community and gathering. For millennia a fire stood as a way for people to meet each other and share their stories, cultures, hopes, and beliefs.

What many people did not seem to realize was the unfortunate fact that a fire was also a point of danger. More so than the aspect of burning someone or something. It was a danger, a beacon, drawing the eyes of those you can't see. Predators in the night; natural animals, humans, shifters...myself.

I shook my head as I watched the human below me.

She was a persistent one, I could give her that. Stupid. Ignorant. Completely unaware of the world she now lived in, and unwilling to realize that. But persistent. A quality I was not sure how I felt about.

I used to think it was an admirable trait; persistence. But now, I realized just how much danger came with it when one did not know when to stop.

The wind shifted again, drawing my attention out of my thoughts.

My head swung to the left, slightly tilting as I smelled the air and tried to filter out the smoke smell.

Someone was coming, hunting the girl, and the human below me was completely unaware.

I growled under my breath, too low for anyone to hear. Normally I wouldn't concern myself with random human matters, but I was pretty sure this particular problem may be one of my doing. I could not be the reason why people were looking for her but leave her unaware and alone after it backfired.

Though, I was not the person who had concocted a plan to send a stranger to kidnap someone who did not need help.

She made it seem so simple; so necessary. It was not what she made it seem to be at all. But, after watching from the shadows when it all went down, I realized she also did not purposefully try to mislead me. I had heard the rumors, the stories, of sky travelers from the past. But I didn't realize the truth behind them until now.

Now I better understood what the girl had been thinking when she came to me. A stranger to our world, terrified and alone. Not knowing why everyone acted, spoke, and made decisions the way they did.

Though I was of this day and age, I too had asked those questions many times in my life.

I was not sure if I simply needed to repay her for what I inadvertently caused or if we were kindred spirits. But I could at least help her save herself.

I inhaled deeply, focusing my senses on the location of the human hunting the girl. Just then, though, the wind shifted and I couldn't catch a scent. Couldn't smell and couldn't see because I was up in a tree, so I could only rely on my hearing.

One set of footprints, treading lightly on the ground. I can pretty much guarantee it was a male, but this person seemed either to be a shifter or have some kind of training for hunting because they knew how to move almost silently throughout the woods.

Which meant the human girl below me most likely could *not* fight him off, but maybe I could get her to run before then.

Leaving over, I silently broke a tiny twig of the branch I still squatted on. Lining it up with a bush on the ground, I threw the twig as hard as I could. Using my shifter power, I managed to get the twig to make a loud enough noise to draw her attention.

The girl shot up and whispered, "Who's there?"

I rolled my eyes and gave a small huff. What kind of idiocy was that? Who asks who is there when they are trying to hide from people.

This time I broke off a bigger branch and snapped it in half, right where I was. Hoping she'd get smarter.

I mean, yeah, I kind of was the reason why she was in this position. But the situation also was not what she made it out to be. So we were pretty even. I would feel perfectly fine leaving her to fend for herself after this if she just used *some* common sense and figured out she should run.

I growled. *This girl.* That time she just started turning around in different directions and throwing threats out.

That was nice. She was now threatening an enemy she couldn't see with weapons she didn't have. If this was how everyone acted in the past, no wonder the world turned out the way it did.

I raised a hand to my temple, messaging the headache I was beginning to get. How can one person be so strong-willed and stupid all at the same time?

My head tilted to the side suddenly as I caught another sound.

The hunter was moving fast and getting closer. I groaned. It seemed like I would have to make a decision and do something more than stay hidden.

Standing on the branch, I grabbed the branch above me. Then I stepped off the branch and dropped, grabbing another branch and using the momentum to swing myself around the other branches and then to the ground.

I landed in a crouch next to the fire, my hand touching the ground to help keep my balance.

I can see the girl stumble back and her mouth open. I lunged forward real fast and threw my hand over her mouth, keeping her from screaming.

I growled out low enough for only her to hear. "What is with you humans? How many times does it take for me to try and make you run for you to do so...and why would you ever ask who is there?" I roll my eyes and shake my head. "Now don't make a sound, what I was trying to tell you is someone is tracking you. You need to leave."

I turn away from her and stomp out the fire, letting the darkness flood back around us.

"Hey! What are you doing? I need that! Now I can't see a thing."

I huffed and turned towards her, "Yea and now other people can't see you. I swear, common sense. The fire draws predators, you know."

I began to gather all of her stuff, then kicked leaves over where the fire had been.

"Oh. Wait, what are you doing now? What are you even doing here?" The girl was talking so much. *Too much.*

I shoved her bag to her chest, then grabbed her arm and began pulling her through the trees.

"I'm saving you, that's what. I had much better things to be doing, but you just couldn't do it yourself."

"Hey! I can handle myself."

I scoffed, "Sure. Now be quiet. Geez, even humans can hear you with all the noise you're making."

I continued to pull her until I was sure she'd keep up with me, without me pulling her. We went until I stopped, holding up my hand for her to stop.

"Shh," I said when she tried to talk. My head tilted as I tried to listen and find where the person was. I didn't hear anything but that didn't mean anything either. "Okay, we will keep going until there's a place I'm sure is far enough for the night. I'll watch over you for the night then let you go on your way tomorrow."

"Wait, what? No. You can't leave me. Please," she began to beg. Almost hysterically.

I shook my head, "Listen. I'm a lone wolf, I guess you can say. I help people, I get them in place, and then I leave. I don't do baggage, friends, or partners. There is no *us.*"

Just like that, I ended up with a stray.